Hitting

Glory

HITTING GLORY

Robert Skead, Hitting Glory

ISBN 1-929478-30-5

Cross Training Publishing
317 West Second Street
Grand Island, NE 68801
(308) 384-5762

Published by Cross Training Publishing,
317 West Second Street
Grand Island, NE 68801
1-800-430-8588
www.crosstrainingpublishing.com

"The pitcher has got only a ball.
I've got a bat.
So the percentage in
weapons is in my favor,
and I let the fellow
with the ball do the fretting."

Hank Aaron

For Robbie:
Who turned what was
becoming stone into a heart again.
And Kirsten:
Whose smile and laugh melts
my heart everyday.

Contents

CHAPTER ONE
Batter Up!

Mrs. Troast delivered her presentation on the Revolutionary War to her sixth grade class with the same skill and style she applied every day. Then, in the middle of a sentence on The Boston Tea Party, she did something she had never done in 20 years of teaching—she snorted.

The rough, noisy sound that came forcefully out when she exhaled through her nostrils started a wave of laughter throughout her class of eleven and twelve-year-olds. One by one, row by row, each boy and girl burst out with giggles. The laughing flowed through the room like a wave.

Lou Gibson, a short, chunky boy with curly black hair seated in the back row, laughed the loudest.

Mrs. Troast's forty-year-old face turned bright red. She quickly adjusted her half-moon glasses and put her hands on her slim hips. Everyone in the class knew that when Mrs. Troast did this, she meant business. The students immediately sat up straight and paid attention. Every one, that is, except Lou.

Lou replayed the snorting scene again in his mind. He

imagined Mrs. Troast's face turning into the face of a pig as she snorted, and he burst out laughing again.

"Excuse me, Mr. Gibson," Mrs. Troast interrupted. "We all had a good laugh. This time, at my expense. I don't think…"

Suddenly, Lou's laugh turned into a melody of uncontrollable giggles as he replayed the snort once again in his mind.

Mrs. Troast's eyes widened with anger. Every kid in the entire class turned around and looked at him.

"Lou, cut it out," whispered Daniel Eng, Lou's best friend. Daniel was taller than Lou, and his black hair was cut like a box around his face.

"Is there a problem Mr. Gibson?" Mrs. Troast asked, her arms crossed. Her face was still red. Only now it was not from embarrassment.

"No. Umm… There's no problem." Lou answered. Lou couldn't control himself and giggled again. *Stop… laughing!* He reprimanded himself in his head. He looked at Mrs. Troast as if to say, "I'm sorry." Then, another laugh spilled out of his mouth. "I'm sorry," he burst with a giggle. "I can't stop." Lou grabbed his stomach hoping that putting pressure on his belly might stop the giggling, but it didn't work. Another round of laughter exploded from his mouth.

"That's enough, Mr. Gibson. You will stay after school and do a service project today. Maybe that thought will help you control your laughter." Mrs. Troast turned her attention back to the chalkboard and to her lesson on The Boston Tea Party.

Lou took a deep breath and gained self-control. He was empty of laughs at last. He sank in his seat and stared back at Mrs. Troast and the 32 other pairs of eyes still staring at him. *Oh, man. What have I done?* Lou locked eyes with Lizandra Collins. Lizandra's strikingly beautiful face revealed a look of total disgust, as if to say "you are *so-o-o* immature."

"You're such a loser, Gibson." It was Justin Rivers. He said it loud enough so everyone in the class could hear. Justin shook his handsome face grimly.

Heads shook with disbelief, and some with gratitude for the pleasant distraction from the schoolwork, as everyone looked ahead at Mrs. Troast and the chalkboard.

Lou looked over at his friend Daniel who rolled his eyes. *How do I get myself into these things?* Lou asked himself. Lou's thoughts then turned to the service project that awaited him. *My afternoon is ruined now. What's she going to have me do? Clean every chalkboard in the school and the erasers too? Clean bathrooms? I refuse to clean toilets. Maybe she'll have me write "I will not get the giggles in class" one million times?* Lou wished he had the answers to the questions.

"Why do you think The Boston Tea Party was such an important event leading to the Revolutionary War? Mr. Gibson." It was Mrs. Troast.

Lou sank lower in his seat. He didn't have the answer to that question, either.

Lou reported to the janitor's office as instructed by Mrs. Troast. Lou was thankful that Mrs. Troast would not be the one deciding the actual work of his service project. Even though she was one of his favorite teachers because she cared so much about each and every one of her students, she was well known as a tough disciplinarian. Lou was scared what she might make him do for disrupting her class.

11

Lou's school, Public School 132 in New York City, started the "Service Project Program" two years ago as a way of helping fix problem behaviors as well as things around the school that were broken. Mr. Broom, the janitor, would be much more merciful than Mrs. Troast, Lou thought.

However, there was still one problem. Mr. Broom was the janitor, which he knew from prior experience meant that this project was going to be a dirty job. *I hope this doesn't involve bathrooms. Why couldn't she have sent me to the gym teacher?*

Lou knocked on the door to Mr. Broom's office, which was in the bowels of the building—in the basement under the gymnasium. It was dark, dusty and there was a constant loud humming noise from the building's boiler down the hall. Lou looked around and envisioned a thousand nasty jobs that could be awaiting him.

The door opened. "Well, hello Lou. How are you today?" Mr. Broom muttered. "Sorry, stupid question… If you're here, that means you're having a bad day." Mr. Broom's smile was bright, and it helped perk Lou up. He wore a tan uniform with his name embroidered on a patch over his chest.

"This isn't one of my best days, but I've had worse," Lou replied.

"Well, don't worry. I won't make it any worse for you. I have to give you a job to do. That's the rules, but what I have in mind isn't that bad. I heard about what happened, and I think I have a punishment to match the crime. Once you get those giggles, it's hard to stop."

"Tell me about it." Lou grinned.

Mr. Broom laughed and led Lou inside. "I'm cleaning

out an old storage room. We just have to move some metal shelving units. They aren't very heavy, so the two of us can handle it. But they're pretty dusty, so you're gonna get dirty. I can find a smock or something for you so you don't get your shirt messed up."

"That's okay. I already spilled milk on it during lunch." Lou said as he followed Mr. Broom into the next room.

"There they are. I took everything off them. They just need to be moved to the other wall, and we'll be in business." Mr. Broom walked over to the gray, metal shelves, which were caked with dust and decorated with cobwebs. "These things haven't been moved probably in a hundred years."

Lou grabbed hold of one end of the unit and Mr. Broom onto the other. Lou pressed his chest against the shelf and inhaled dust. He sneezed. So did Mr. Broom. "God bless you," they said simultaneously.

They chuckled and continued to push the unit forward. Just then, Lou heard a noise and felt his foot kick something. His heart skipped a beat not knowing what gross, old thing was by his side—or if it were alive or dead. He looked down, and there it was—a baseball bat.

"Heyyyy. Look at this." Lou bent down and slowly picked up the dusty, old, brown bat.

"You wouldn't believe the things I find in this place," Mr. Broom stated as he saw Lou lift the bat from the floor. "Some kid probably left it here. That probably rolled off the shelf years ago."

Lou dusted off the barrel of the bat with his hand revealing a circular logo that read "Spalding." He then noticed a large mark on the barrel of the bat where the wood's natural grain created a black spot. The distinctive

13

mark was the size of a silver dollar. Lou wiped his dusty, blackened hand on his shirt. "This is so cool." Lou's eyes and smile widened with delight, and he hoped the tone of his voice would convince Mr. Broom to let him keep it.

"It looks just about your size," Mr. Broom observed. "Whoever owned that old thing is surely dead and gone by now. Tell you what… consider it yours." Mr. Broom added, knowing his words would make Lou happy.

"Really? Thanks!" Lou dusted the bat off some more with the bottom of his shirt and gripped the handle like a hitter. The bat was his size. Lou didn't know why, but the bat felt different, like there was something extraordinary or special about it. His hands tingled while holding it, and goose bumps formed on his arms.

Mr. Broom smiled at Lou remembering the days when he played baseball. He scratched his balding head. "I don't know how old that thing is, but you could probably still use it," he said. "It's cool and dry down here. Good conditions to keep that old wood from spoiling. You know, that bat represents good, old fashioned, made in the USA crafts-manship. Yep, I bet that bat still has *a lot* of hits in it," he said playfully.

Lou glanced around the room to make sure there was room for a practice swing. He took a swing and laughed. "This is like the perfect bat. The length… the weight…"

"That's a pretty good swing you have there." Mr. Broom nodded.

"Thanks, 'Homerun' is my middle name."

"Really?"

"I wish. Actually my name is 'Foul Tip.' That's because usually I'm lucky if I just get my bat on the ball." Lou paused and took another cut. "Too bad it's not aluminum, or I'd use it."

"Aluminum bats are the worst thing to ever happen to baseball," Mr. Broom proclaimed with the passion of a baseball purist. "Now, if you don't mind, let's get this job finished so we can both go home."

"You bet." Lou smiled and placed the bat gently in the corner of the room. As he lifted the remaining units of shelves, he couldn't help but feel thankful for his episodes of giggling earlier in the day. Even though it caused him some embarrassment, he now owned a very cool and old baseball bat as a result.

CHAPTER TWO
Discoveries

The service project only took 20 minutes to complete, and Lou and his new (or old) bat were on their way home. As Lou exited the building into the strong daylight, he glanced again at the Spalding logo. It read "A.G. Spalding & Bros. Trade Mark" and was shaped like a baseball.

Lou slid the bat through his hand and held it at the bottom of the handle. He looked at the bottom of the bat and noticed some lettering. He stopped and dusted it off. The caked on dust didn't come off easily. Lou spit on his finger and rubbed the dirt off hard, revealing two initials carved on the bottom of the bat. Lou's eyes widened with surprise. The initials were the same as his—LG. Lou laughed and his smile grew from ear to ear. It was as if the bat was meant to be his.

Lou took a few steps forward then stopped dead in his tracks. His heart began racing. He looked at the initials again to see if they were indeed the same as his. They were. *Oh my… It can't be!* The bat was old, really old. *That could mean…* Lou then remembered that his school, Public

School 132, had a very famous graduate—Lou Gehrig! The Pride of the Yankees!

This could be his bat! This could be Lou Gehrig's bat! Lou wanted to yell the words, but he bit his tongue. He casually put the bat to his side. He knew that if it were true, the bat might be worth a lot of money, and he didn't want anyone to steal it. Lou looked around the busy street to see if anyone was watching. *Good. No one's looking.* He then gripped the bat tightly with all his might and moved on down the street.

"How many people with the initials LG could there have been at PS 132?" he asked himself. *Probably a lot... And if there were a lot of LGs, how many were baseball players?* Questions soared through Lou's mind at a million miles per second on how to determine who the LG represented. *This is all so weird. Lou Gehrig was one of baseball's best.*

Lou wanted to tell someone, but realized he couldn't—not yet. He had to determine if this was really Lou Gehrig's bat or not. *But how?*

Lou slowly opened the door to his apartment and listened for any sign of his mom. The rather drab-looking dwelling showed a lack of fine furniture and ornate knick-knacks. There was also a lack of noise. *Ah. The coast is clear. And better yet—I don't have to explain why I'm late.* Lou had rehearsed the reason for his tardy arrival just seconds before he entered the door. His mind was consumed with the bat in his hand, but he realized he could not focus his attention on finding out who its owner was if he were grounded by his mom, so he had a good story planned. He was going to tell the truth—that he was home late because he was helping Mr. Broom the janitor. He would strategically omit why he had to help Mr. Broom.

Lou ran to his room and hid the bat in his closet. His first mission would be to determine the age of the bat. That would let him know if the bat could have belonged to Lou Gehrig or not. He remembered the tingling feeling in his hands and the goose bumps on his arms when he held the bat. It has to be his, he thought.

Lou turned on his computer, which used to be his Dad's, and mapped out a plan in his mind as he waited for it to boot up. He noticed the picture on his desk of his father holding him when he was a baby. Suddenly, he was gripped by sadness. I would love to tell you about this, he thought.

When the wallpaper on his computer appeared, which was an image of the New York Yankees logo, he immediately refocused and double clicked on the Internet. *I'll do a search on Spalding baseball bats. Hopefully, there will be a history page or some old examples with pictures and dates.*

Lou searched the Internet for half an hour and found nothing very useful. In his quest to identify the bat, he did learn some interesting information along the way. He discovered that there were two types of bats in the old days—bottle bats and mushroom bats. Bottle bats were in the shape of a bottle and had thick handles. Mushroom bats had a distinctive, mushroom shape knob handle. It was cheaper for bat manufacturers to leave the knob on rather than cut it off. That information was cool, but as he continued his search, he needed specific information on Spalding bats. His last sources for information brought him to an auction site. With a dozen more clicks, there it was—an old Spalding baseball bat for sale by a collector!

Lou ran to his closet and took out the bat. He compared the logo on the barrel to that on the screen. They were identical. Lou's heart skipped a beat and his palms grew sweaty. The description paragraph stated that the bat's logo revealed that it was manufactured in the years 1900—1915, which meant that the same held true for Lou's bat. "Yes! The bat's old! This is awesome! I should be a detective!" Lou exclaimed. Lou read on and learned that the Spalding logo had changed over the years. The logo on his bat changed in the year 1919.

His next mission was to find out more about Lou Gehrig and see if he was in elementary school during that time period. This part was easy, and in a matter of clicks, he discovered an entire listing of Lou Gehrig information, complete with biographies and career statistics.

Lou discovered that Gehrig was born on June 19, 1903. He added twelve years, the age of most of the kids in his grade, to 1903, and the result was 1915. "Yes!" Lou jumped out of his seat and started to pace. "That would put Gehrig in elementary school from about 1910 - 1917."

"Honey! I'm home!" It was Lou's mom. She was short and plump with a pleasant face and a kindly nature. Mrs. Gibson entered the apartment door, placed her pocket book on the kitchen counter and headed for Lou's room.

Lou immediately picked up his bat and hid it in his closet.

"Hi, honey. How was school?" she asked as she popped her head in through the doorway. She was still wearing the grocery store uniform, which had her first name embroidered over her heart—Dolores.

"Oh! Fine." Lou replied casually, trying to conceal his excitement as he stood in front of his closet.

Lou's mom looked at the computer screen curiously. "You doing homework early?" she asked. Lou was usually having a snack in the kitchen, watching TV or out playing with friends at this time of the day.

Lou glanced toward the computer, which now displayed his outer space screen saver. "Umm…. Kinda," he replied. "I'm, ah, doing some research."

"That's nice, honey," she said, barely paying attention. She leaned against the door jamb exhausted. "Research is important if you're gonna be success…" She yawned. "…ful." She yawned again. "Dinner will be in 20 minutes."

"Okay." Lou gave his mom an anxious look that revealed he wanted to get back to what he was doing.

Lou's mom started out the door, then… "What's that all over your shirt?" Her tired voice turned serious. "I'm working two jobs to help us get by so you can have decent clothes. That shirt is practically new."

"It's second hand."

"It's new to you, and it still costs money. How'd it get so dirty?"

Lou glanced down at his shirt casually. "I was helping Mr. Broom, the janitor at school."

Lou's mom yawned again.

Lou took the pause as an opportunity to change the subject. He stood up. "And look what I found while I was helping him." Lou opened his closet and took out the bat.

"That's nice," she stated, unimpressed. "You already have a bat," his mom added.

"But this one is old, really old, and I think…" he stopped himself. "I think… it's really, really old." Lou offered it to his mom as if she might like to take a swing with it.

"I'm going to go get dinner ready, all right? And do me a favor…"

Lou straightened up attentively.

"Change your shirt before you come to the table." She left.

Lou took a deep breath. *Whew.* He then quickly returned his eyes to his computer and read more about his hero. He learned that Gehrig's favorite player was Honus Wagner, a famous shortstop in the early 1900s and that Gehrig liked him because he was also a German immigrant. He also confirmed that Gehrig did indeed attend his school—PS 132—and that he went on to Commerce High School where he never missed a day of school. He then went to Columbia University where he was a star football and baseball player before he became a Yankee.

Lou scrolled down and found out that Gehrig batted over .300 for 12 straight years, led the American League in home runs three times, led the American League in RBIs five times, and played on six World Championship teams.

Although he had heard about and read about most of this before, it still impressed him. He then read about Gehrig's record of playing in 2,130 consecutive games and that they called Gehrig *The Iron Horse* because of his ability to stay in the lineup. Lou also read how that record stood for years until Cal Ripken of the Baltimore Orioles broke it in 1995.

The biography ended with Gehrig's fight against amyotrophic lateral sclerosis, a rare muscle disease that took his life at the age of 37.

Lou felt sad as he thought about the tragic ending to a brilliant career and man. He walked over to the bat and picked it up. His hands began to tingle and goose bumps formed on his arms. He looked at the LG on the bottom of the handle, then took a walloping swing. He glanced over at the computer screen and the photo of Gehrig. "Is this your bat?" he asked The Iron Horse. He wished the photo could answer.

Lou sat down and then read again the incredible hitting records next to the photo. He wondered how many hits and home runs the young Lou Gehrig might have hit with the bat in his hands.

"I bet that bat still has a lot of hits in it." The words from Mr. Broom earlier in the day echoed inside his head.

Lou felt a surge of energy run through his body as he stood up and swung the bat. He felt as if the bat were a special gift to him from God.

CHAPTER THREE
Foul Tip

The next day, Lou got dressed, ate breakfast and walked to school faster than he ever did in his life. He arrived 15 minutes early, headed straight for the school office and asked the secretary, Mrs. Nelson, if she had any information on Lou Gehrig attending PS 132. She chuckled and told him many people ask her that same question. All she knew was that he graduated from the school in 1917.

Lou asked if there was any way to find Lou Gehrig's school records and a listing of students who attended the school from 1911 to 1917. He was hoping to discover if there were any other students with the initials LG. If there weren't, then the bat must have belonged to Gehrig.

Mrs. Nelson looked at him curiously and referred him to the librarian, Miss Sandy Murcer (who everyone called Miss Sandy) for help.

Lou looked at the large clock on the wall. There were 10 minutes remaining until school officially started, and he had to be in class. He turned on his heels and walked as fast as he could, without actually running, toward the media center.

He was dying to tell his best friend Daniel about what was happening, but he needed to be sure. He looked at his watch—8 minutes until attendance was to be taken. He briskly brushed by student after student.

"Hey, giggler." It was Justin Rivers. He placed his strong body right in front of Lou and blocked his path. "You going to giggle for us today?"

Oh, no. Not now... Lou exhaled a deep breath.

"You know, you sound just like a girl when you giggle." Justin mimicked Lou. "I'm sorry, Mrs. Troast. I can't stop. I got the giggles." The three boys standing with Justin started to laugh.

Lou was speechless. He wanted to say "very funny," but he didn't want anything related to laughing to come out of his mouth. It would only give Justin more ammunition with which to pick on him. He glanced at Justin and the other boys, not looking them in the eye. He wished there was a way to make them stop poking fun at him so he could be on his way. He looked at his watch. Thanks to this disruption, there wouldn't be enough time to meet with Miss Sandy and ask her questions. In an angry tone, Lou said, "Are you done, Justin? I have to get to class," as he took a step forward.

Justin confronted him. "I don't like your tone, Gibson. Someone like you should be a lot nicer to someone like me." Justin laughed. "Or have you forgotten that I struck you out practically every time last year?"

"No, I remember."

"Oh, yeah. You got that bloop single one game that dropped over the second baseman's head. Hardly a real hit."

"I remember that hit. It hit off the end of the bat or

something," declared Andre Robinson with his usual smart-alecky tone. Andre was one of Justin's pals. He was the shortest kid in class but really good at basketball, football and baseball.

"It's still in the books as a hit," Lou said with a cocky and aggressive tone. Suddenly, Lou felt his stomach get upset. He didn't want to start anything, and he knew what he mentioned could lead to a fight.

Justin glared at Lou. "It was a cheap hit. I would have had a 'no hitter' if it weren't for that dinky little hit." Just then, his expression changed. "Not to worry. You won't get a bat on the ball off me this season. And when I make it to the Big Leagues some day, you can tell your kids that you had the honor of getting one hit off me. You won't want to mention all the other strike outs." Justin laughed, along with the other boys.

"Those are pretty big goals," Lou responded, growing tired of the conversation.

"Listen, Mr. Girly Giggler. I guarantee you will not get a bat on the ball when you stand in the batter's box against me. I'll throw nothing but strikes, and they'll be so fast you'll still be swinging when the catcher throws it back to me." Justin puffed out his chest. The name of his baseball team, BRAVES, printed in gold on his blue jersey seemed to grow larger before Lou's eyes. Justin's words were more than a threat. They were said with total confidence as if they were a promise.

"If I keep getting hits off you, I bet he can, too!" echoed a voice from behind. It was Tanya Sanchez. Tanya brushed back her brown hair and put her hand on Lou's shoulder.

Lou looked at Tanya strangely. Tanya was excellent at everything she did—singing, dancing, art, drama—and playing baseball. While all the other girls played softball, Tanya was the only girl that still played baseball with the boys. Lou wasn't friendly with her. He was surprised by what she said—and that her hand was on his shoulder.

"Oh, hi, Tanya." Justin didn't know what else to say, which was a rarity.

Lou smiled with the thought that it took a girl to shut Justin up.

"Hi, Tanya." Andre and the others said enthusiastically at the same time.

Tanya brushed back her shining brown hair with her hand. She knew that the boys loved it when she did that. It gave her some sort of mysterious power over them. She taunted Justin, "You know, whether Lou gets a hit off you or not doesn't matter. A good hitter is considered success-ful if he gets a hit 3 out of 10 times. I'm 6 for 10 off you. Besides, Lou is a great outfielder. Being a good hitter isn't everything."

Lou found himself standing a little taller. He liked hav-ing someone on his side for a change. Although he knew he was a better fielder than a hitter, no one ever called him "great" before. Lou looked at her as if to say "thanks."

Just then, the bell rang. Everyone in the halls began to quickly disperse.

"Get to class, Girly Giggler. We wouldn't want you to be late and have to do another service project. I'll look for-ward to playing you sometime!" Justin brushed by Lou. His pals followed.

Tanya adjusted her backpack and started on her way. Lou wanted to stop her and thank her, but feared being late for attendance. He rushed into his classroom and sat beside Daniel.

"You were almost late," Daniel stated.

"Tell me about it," Lou answered.

As Lou's homeroom teacher, Mrs. Galarce, called attendance, Lou could not help but think that this was not how he wanted his morning to start. Well, at least I don't have to face him on the mound tonight, he thought. Lou quickly turned his thoughts towards the bat and Miss Sandy. Unfortunately, his class-schedule that day was full, and he had a game after school, so he would not be able to get to her until tomorrow.

Lou glanced over at Daniel. *Should I tell him? I could write a note. No. I better wait.* The fact that he had to wait an entire day to see Miss Sandy and that he couldn't tell his best friend about the bat tore him up inside.

Later that afternoon as Lou was getting ready for his game, his mind was still focused totally on the bat. He wondered what it would be worth if it really did belong to Gehrig. The answer, he figured, could be found on the Internet. Within a few minutes, Lou had his computer on and had found a web site belonging to a vintage baseball bat collector. The collector not only displayed some of his old bats on his web site, but also offered some for sale. Lou clicked the "contact" icon and typed this message:

Dear Sir,

My name is Lou Gibson, and I am 11 years old. I was wondering if you could tell me what a Spalding bat belonging to Lou Gehrig from when he was a boy might be worth. Please let me know. Thanks!

Lou Gibson

Lou felt a surge of adrenaline rush through his veins as he hit the send button. He wondered what kind of response he might receive, if he even received one at all.

CHAPTER FOUR
Line Drives

It was a cool afternoon for May. There was a light breeze. It was the perfect day for a baseball game. Lou knelt in the on-deck circle and took it all in. He loved the smell of the freshly-cut grass in the air and the feel of the dirt beneath him. As the pitcher took his warm up, Lou studied his motion. He noticed that the pitcher had great control, which was exceptionally rare for most kids his age. *That's good. I can dig into the batter's box.* Lou also noticed that his fastball didn't have a lot of zip on it. *That's even better. I can place myself up in the box.*

Lou stood up and practiced his swing. The bat he gripped in his hands was a very special bat. The 30" Easton® was a Christmas gift from his mother. She worked overtime for a week just to be able to afford it. Like any gift from a mom to her son, the bat held extra special meaning because of its giver. As Lou took his practice swings, he noticed a vast difference in the way the aluminum bat felt in his hands compared to the old, wooden Spalding.

"Strike three! You're out!" yelled the umpire, as Lou's teammate swung and missed.

He walked dejectedly past Lou towards the dug out.

"Come on, Lou! Be a hitter in there! You can do it!" yelled Lou's Coach, Richard Jeffer, clapping his hands at his position beside third base. Richard was stocky like a football player, and his blonde hair was cut short.

Lou took his stance on the left side of the plate in the middle of the batter's box and dug his back foot in. He bent his knees and balanced his weight on the balls of his feet. He lifted the bat off his shoulder and awaited the pitch.

The pitcher, a skinny red head whose oversized baseball pants flapped in the wind, was already into his wind up. He let the ball fly.

Lou focused his eyes on the ball and in a fraction of a second launched his swing.

"Strike one!" exclaimed the umpire.

Lou missed the pitch, as they say, by a country mile.

"Choke up, Lou!" yelled the coach.

"Hey, it's Mr. Foul Tip! No batter! He's a whiffer!" yelled the shortstop. "No stick!"

Lou felt his confidence shrink. *Come on. Concentrate. Make contact with the ball. Cut the ball in half with the bat.*

"Come on, Lou!" yelled his teammates half-heartedly from the bench. "We need base runners!"

Lou grabbed a handful of dirt. He let it fall from his fingers and rubbed his hands on the bat's handle. He then wiped his hands across the chest of his yellow jersey, which read INDIANS in black. He took his stance in the batter's box, went through his preparation routine and awaited the pitch.

"Hey-batta-batta-batta! He's a whiffer, whiffer, whiffer! He can't hit! No batta! No batta! No batter!" the infield chatted.

The pitcher released the ball. It hurled through the air. Lou could see that it was going to be a perfect strike. He swung.

"Strike two!" added the ump.

"Take this guy now!" yelled the shortstop to the pitcher. "Don't even bother wasting a pitch!"

Lou studied his bat to see if it were invisible or something. He hit the barrel with his hand and shook his head.

"Come on, Lou! Little Bingo, baby! Protect the plate!" yelled Coach Jeffer enthusiastically. "We need you on first!"

Lou leered at the pitcher who looked anxious to strike him out. He then looked over at his teammates watching him from the bench. Everyone was dejectedly reaching for their gloves, anticipating that he would strike out and that the inning would be over. Lou was tired of seeing the look of disappointment in his teammates' eyes whenever he got up to bat. For years he had practiced hard and studied the fundamentals of hitting, but the breaks never seemed to go his way.

"This guy stinks!" the shortstop taunted. "He's Mr. Foul Tip! He's a whiffer! Strike out this loser!"

The words echoed inside Lou's mind. "Whiffer! Loser! Whiffer! Loser! Whiffer…" Each resounding syllable went straight to his heart. *If only I could make them stop.* He turned to the umpire. "Time!" He walked toward the dug out.

Coach Jeffer and everyone on the bench looked at him strangely. "Come on, Lou. Get back in there. You can do it!" the coach yelled, wondering what was going on inside Lou's head.

"Hey, what's wrong?" It was Daniel. He asked what the entire bench was thinking.

Lou didn't answer, but walked straight to his

33

equipment bag. He unzipped the end, reached carefully inside and slowly pulled out the old, wooden Spalding baseball bat. A smile formed on his face as he felt his hands begin to tingle and goose bumps form on his arms. *Ah.*

"What is that?" exclaimed Bobby Darby, the team's third baseman. "You're gonna use a wooden bat?"

Everyone on the bench traded looks of mutual inquiry and laughed, even Daniel.

"No one uses wood anymore! You can't hit with aluminum. You're not going to do any better with that old thing," said Bobby seriously. "Use my bat if you don't like yours. Come on man, this is a big game."

Lou ignored his invitation—and everyone's laughter—and headed for the plate.

Coach Jeffer clapped. He was thankful Lou was not giving up. "Come on now, Louie kid! Big hit now! Wait for your pitch and protect the plate."

Lou took his stance in the batter's box.

The umpire smiled as he noticed the wooden stick in Lou's hands. It was as if he was looking at an old friend.

The catcher saw the bat, too, and shook his head as he positioned his glove in the center of the strike zone.

Lou gently reached down and touched the corner of the plate with the end of his bat. He positioned his feet and bent his knees. A deep-exhale came forth from his mouth and a relaxing feeling overcame his body. His hands tingled as he raised the Spalding off his shoulder. In came the pitch.

"Ball! Outside!" proclaimed the umpire.

The catcher threw the ball back to the pitcher. The routine started again. Lou readied himself. His weight was balanced. His hands still tingled. The pitch was delivered.

Lou gripped the bat tighter, and swung the bat's barrel over the plate and—

WHAM!

The ball went screaming right over the pitcher's head for a line drive base hit into center field.

Lou's heart raced with excitement as he ran toward first base and rounded the bag.

The center fielder threw the ball into the infield, and Lou went back to the base and stood proudly upon the bag.

Suddenly, everyone began laughing.

Lou looked down at his hand—the object of their laughter. He was still holding his bat.

"He's so surprised he got a hit, he forgot to let go of his bat!" the shortstop hollered.

The comment caused Lou's teammates to laugh as well.

Lou smiled, not because of what was said, but because he got a hit. Not only did he hit the ball, he hit it with authority. He handed the bat to Mr. Tilly, the first base coach. "Hold this for me, please. And don't let anyone touch it, okay?"

"No problem," he replied. Mr. Tilly had thick black hair, and his dark skin was almost as rough as his belt. As he took hold of the bat, a thousand memories went through his mind from the days when he played with a wooden bat.

The next four at bats proved equally successful for Lou. He hit two more singles, then a double and a triple, going 5 for 5. Lou managed to let go of the bat after each hit. However, instead of throwing the bat, he gently let it fall to the ground. The Indians beat the Marlins 9 to 3. After the game, everyone, including Lou, was astonished about his hitting performance.

"Let me see that," said Calvin Welling, the catcher, with a tone that suggested he'd never use it, as he grabbed the bat.

"Hey, careful…" exclaimed Lou, not liking how it was taken. "It's old."

"It looks ancient, man." Calvin inspected the bat like it was an artifact from a museum. "Where'd you get this thing?" Calvin asked.

Lou paused. "Um. I, ah, umm… got it from a friend. A friend gave it to me."

"What's that? Black paint on the barrel?" asked Calvin.

"No. It's a knot in the wood," said Lou impatiently.

"I'd never use it," stated Frank Anderson, the second baseman, as if it were a fact. Frank was handsome, his long brown hair feathered out from underneath his hat. "The ball will go a lot farther with an aluminum bat. No offense, but you're lucky you got a hit at all with that old thing."

Lou took the bat back quickly from Calvin so no one else could hold it. "Yeah, well, the rules say we can use wood or aluminum bats." Lou turned his attention to Coach Jeffer. "Right, Coach?"

"That's right. It's every player's choice," the coach admitted.

"It worked for me today, so I'm going to use it." Lou felt the tingling sensation in his hands disappear as he placed the bat gently back inside his equipment bag.

"Lou, you had a great game out there today, which is why I'm awarding you the game ball." Coach Jeffer tossed a baseball to Lou. "Five for five, three singles, a double and a triple, with six RBIs… You certainly deserve it."

Coaches Jeffer and Tilly applauded along with a few other players.

"You never showed me that bat before," whispered Daniel so no one could hear.

"Some other time. Not now," Lou whispered back.

"Next game is against the Tigers, fellas!" Coach Jeffer hollered as his team began to pack their belongings and disperse. "Be here at 5:30 sharp. No excuses!"

Lou's smile widened as he held the game ball. It was the first one he ever received. He looked at the ball and imagined himself writing his game statistics on it and placing it on his dresser. *This has got to be Lou Gehrig's bat. There's not a doubt in my mind, but I'm still gonna prove it.*

CHAPTER FIVE
The Challenge

Miss Sandy sat behind her desk and quietly listened to Lou's request for specific information on Gehrig. The library was extremely silent, and Lou spoke softly not wanting anyone else to hear him. Lou asked if there was any way to confirm the dates Gehrig attended PS 132 and if there was a way to find out if any other students had the initials LG during the time Gehrig was at the school.

"So, can you help?" Lou's eyes practically begged for a positive answer.

Miss Sandy smiled. Immediately, her mind began to search for possible ways to fulfill Lou's large, and strange, request. She scratched her chin. "Is this for a report?" she asked. Her inquisitive brown eyes were just a shade lighter than her hair.

Lou froze. "Well, um… No, it's not for a report, but it's for a very special project I'm working on. I might do a report on it when I'm done." Lou started tapping his yellow pencil on the desk.

"Oh," she replied. She rubbed her hands together as

she thought. "Finding out the dates Lou Gehrig went to school here shouldn't be too difficult. I'm sure somebody around here knows, or it's got to be in a book somewhere. To find out other students during that time with the initials LG... Well, that will be hard. I'd have to dig back into some really old files that may not even be stored in this building anymore." She sighed, thinking of the work ahead of her. "I don't know..."

Lou's heart began to sink.

Miss Sandy looked into Lou's eyes and noticed a hint of desperation. "Oh, all right. I'll do it. It'll be a challenge. And I love a good challenge and a good research project," she stated, knowing this meant a lot to the young boy before her.

"Yes!" Lou yelled. He threw his hand into the air. "Thank you so much!" He was so elated he wanted to kiss her pretty face.

"Shhhhhhhhhhhhhhhhhhhhhhhhhhh," said a symphony of pursed lips throughout the room sounding like a slew of snakes. Eyes glared at Lou.

"Ooops... Sorry," murmured Lou, his face red with embarrassment. He leaned in closer to Miss Sandy. "Thank you," he whispered.

Miss Sandy nodded. "Don't thank me yet," she replied with an equally quiet whisper. "I haven't found out any-thing."

"Nice game yesterday, Gibson!" It was Calvin.

He playfully hit Lou on the shoulder with his fist as he walked down the hall.

"Thanks," replied Lou. His face was lit up like a Christmas tree. He continued down the hall toward his next class. *Nice game... Never heard that one before.*

"Hey! I heard what you did yesterday, Lou. Way to go," exclaimed Tanya Sanchez enthusiastically. She held up her hand for a high five, and Lou slapped it. "You the man! I knew you had it in you." Tanya brushed back her hair, smiled and winked at him, then walked on through the crowd.

I could get used to this. Lou found his head turning and his eyes following Tanya as he walked, then…

"Ow! Look where you're going! Loser."

Lou suddenly locked eyes with Justin Rivers. *Oh, no. Not again…*

"You stepped on my foot, Giggler Girl. You're such a klutz!" Justin shook his head impatiently.

"Sorry."

"That's the toughest thing you can say?" Justin glanced to his left and right and acknowledged the students who were watching.

Lou paused. "Sorry… Jerk." Lou caught Justin's eye and glanced away. He knew immediately in his heart that he should not have said that. His mom had been teaching him the importance of self-control and doing what was right. It was part of her plan to train her son for success and for a life that put others first. *Ah! Self-control!*

"What'd you say?" Justin's face was inches from Lou.

Think fast. You made a mistake. Now get out of it. Think smart. What would Mom do? Lord, help me… "Um…. Yeah… I called you a jerk. You… ah… gotta agree that's what you've been acting like. All I did was bump into you and step on your toe. That was hardly reason for you to insult me."

"You're a klutz." Justin didn't expect a rebuttal, and he searched for words as well.

"So, I said I was sorry. You couldn't just leave it at that?"

"Nnnn-o." Justin stammered.

"Why not?"

"Why? You wanna know why?" Justin paused. His heart beat like a drum in his chest.

"Yeah." Lou lied.

"Because I don't like you, Gibson. I never have. I think you stink at sports. I think you're not very smart. I think you have big, goofy ears. I think you wear stupid clothes. Basically, I think you're a loser, a mommy's boy, who can't even afford a cool pair of sneakers. And you know what? Lots of people in this school think the *same* thing," Justin stated matter of factly. "That's why you don't have any friends."

Lou didn't know what to say. Each statement seemed to pierce his heart and soul. Tears welled up in his eyes.

Justin noticed Lou's lip quiver. "Look. You're about to cry because I told you the truth."

A tear ran uncontrollably down Lou's cheek.

"Just like a momma's boy to cry. Where's your daddy anyway, Gibson?"

Lou wouldn't answer. He just stood there frozen, speechless.

Many of the students stared at Justin, shook their heads and walked away.

"That's what I think about you, Gibson. You have nothing to say?" Justin started to walk away.

Lou's body started to tremble. He felt wounded. He wanted to run home to his mom and be in her arms. *I guess I am a momma's boy.* He wiped the tears from his face with his sleeve and tried not to notice those who were staring at him. He looked down the hall a few feet and glared at

Justin, who laughed and high-fived one of his pals. *Self-control... Self-control...*

Justin looked back and shot Lou a look of disdain. Lou hated the expression in Justin's eyes.

"Hey! You know what Rivers?" Lou yelled.

Justin turned his head toward Lou.

"I can hit anything you throw at me." Lou couldn't believe what came out of his mouth. He thought about his new special baseball bat and the feeling he had when he held it. He felt braver. "And I'll bet the next time I face you I'll put more hits in the score book. Maybe I'll even hit one out of the park! And I do think you're a jerk."

Justin shook his head and laughed. "That's an even bigger joke than you are! You just don't know when to stop, do you?" He walked up and got in Lou's face. "You will *never* get a hit off me again. I promise. Tell ya what, Gibson... I'll even put my money where my mouth is. If you ever so much as get a bat on the ball off me that is more than a 'foul tip'... I'll buy you a new pair of sneakers, name brand just like mine—and these cost a lot of money!"

"I don't think he's ever had a pair of new sneakers." Andre laughed. Others joined him. Justin patted his friend on the back and walked into class.

Lou stood in the hallway alone. His nose was runny. He wanted to go home.

Mrs. Galarce wrote a new math problem on the chalkboard. I don't get this, Lou thought to himself as he sat behind his desk in class. He couldn't concentrate on anything that was being taught, although he tried hard. The good feeling that he had since yesterday's game was gone. All he could think about were Justin's words and the fact that others may think of him the same way.

43

As much as he wanted to, he couldn't make himself focus on anything else during the rest of the school day. After the final bell had rung, Lou gathered his books and nonchalantly targeted the door. He walked through the crowd, but talked to no one. Not even to those who said hello to him. In a matter of minutes, he was on the busy city-street where he blended in with the crowd. His only saving grace, he felt, was that soon he would see his mom. If Daniel Eng was Lou's best friend, Dolores Gibson was Lou's "best-est" friend. And he longed to hear her gentle, loving voice.

Lou ran up to his apartment, took out his key and unlocked the door. "Mom! I'm home!" He dropped his backpack and waited for a reply. There was no answer.

He went into the kitchen and poured himself a glass of juice. After he grabbed a pretzel rod, he went to his room. Sitting neatly upon his bed was a pile of freshly washed clothes. Lou stared at them like they were dirty old rags. *He's right. They are stupid looking.* For the first time in his life, Lou felt self-conscious about his clothing, and he wished he had some money so he could buy "cool" clothes. He walked toward his desk and tripped over one of his dress shoes that was thrown on the floor. *Man... I am a klutz.*

Lou looked at himself in the mirror and wanted to cry again. His dislike of Justin Rivers was turning into hate. He didn't like the emotion that stirred deep inside. He knew that feeling hate toward anyone was wrong and that he had to deal with it.

Lou caught a glimpse of the game ball sitting proudly on his dresser. He picked it up, studied the hand-written stats and smiled, reminded of his accomplishment. *The bat!* Lou opened his closet, grabbed his equipment bag and

44

slowly took out the old Spalding baseball bat. The tingling sensation ran from his hands up his arms and into his heart. Lou knew he had plenty to be thankful for, but he felt as if the bat were the only good thing in his life right now.

E-mail! I wonder if that guy responded yet? Lou laid the bat down on his bed and turned on his computer. He anxiously tapped on his desk while he waited for his computer to boot up. He logged on to his Internet access provider and noticed he had mail.

One click revealed five new messages. The third one was from batdude7@oldbats.com. Lou's heart raced as he quickly clicked on it:

> Dear Lou,
>
> Thanks for visiting my site. I love to hear that young people like yourself are interested in baseball and in collecting. It is a fun hobby!
>
> Now, regarding your question. To my knowledge (and I did some research) no such bat exists. However, if it did exist, it would most certainly be a rare, one of a kind item. With that in mind, I will speculate on a price for you, just for fun. Keep in mind that the memorabilia market is always an uncertainty, based on perceptions and emotions. Since your question involves a Hall of Famer like Gehrig, it will be easier to estimate because he will always be a popular icon. Sorry, I digress, but I like to educate young hobby enthusiasts. A bat like the one you described could be worth anywhere from $10,000 to $15,000, if it existed. As with everything in the collecting world, price depends also on condition. If a bat is cracked, has wood that is

spreading or splitting, or if there are lots of nicks and dents in a bat, then the price becomes dramatically lower.

You should also know about the law of supply and demand—the lesser the supply, the greater the demand. The more rare something is—the more it's worth.

In the memorabilia market, people have been known to pay a lot of money for something that other people wouldn't even buy for one dollar. Recently, someone bought a bat that Babe Ruth leaned on the day his number was retired for over one hundred thousand dollars! I guess what I'm trying to say is that values are always difficult to determine. What I might perceive as valuable, someone else may not and vice versa.

I hope that helps! Feel free to contact me anytime!

Harry Halperin

"Wow! If it's real, it could be worth $15,000!" Lou forgot all about his other e-mails and picked up the bat from the bed. As the tingling sensation ran up and down his arms, his mind turned to his hitting. *Do I go for the glory? What if the bat breaks? It could be worthless? We could sure use the money? But if it's not Gehrig's bat, whether it breaks or not doesn't matter.* Lou didn't know what to do.

He plopped down on his bed. As he lay there, he thought about the bat and his life. His thoughts turned to his mom. Even though she worked two jobs, which still didn't pay all the bills on time or provide for everything he wanted, she was always there for him when he had a problem. *If the bat did belong to him, I could sell it. That would make things a lot easier for Mom.*

Later that evening, Lou realized that his mom had come home early and that something was wrong. He wanted to talk to her and find out what had happened. He also wanted to talk to her about what was happening in his life, but he wasn't quite sure what to say or how to say it. So many feelings, so many thoughts, ran through his being. As he reflected, he felt the words forming on his tongue. So he got out of bed and walked to her room.

Lou smiled at the sight of her reading, tucked comfortably inside her covers. "Mom."

"Hi." She gracefully put her book down on her lap.

Lou entered slowly and sat beside her. There was silence for a moment as she stroked his hair.

"Mom… what's wrong?"

His mom paused not wanting to talk about it. She looked deeply into her son's eyes and saw the look of real concern. "They made an announcement today that they're cutting back everyone's overtime hours. That means I have to find a new job… but don't worry; I'll find one."

Lou wished that there was something he could say that would cheer her up. "Mom, remember that bat I found?"

"Yeah."

"I… I got five hits with it last game."

"That's great, honey." She paused. "How come you're not using the bat I gave you for Christmas?"

Lou glanced away, not knowing what to say. He didn't want to hurt her feelings. "Um… I… I just wasn't playing that well with it." His eyes lit up with excitement. "This bat…" He stopped himself.

"What?"

"Nothing."

Lou's mom stretched her arms and yawned. She placed her hand on her son's knee. "You warm enough? It's supposed to get cold tonight. Why don't you put some pajama bottoms on instead of those silly old boxer shorts."

"Mo-mmmm," Lou whined.

"I'm sorry. I- ah- I know you're old enough to know when to change. It's just..."

"I know... I'm a momma's boy."

"That's not what I was going to say. I don't know what I was going to say." She laughed. "Besides, you're *not* a momma's boy, but you are Momma's boy. If you know what I mean?"

Lou smiled understanding the sentiment.

He paused, then- "Mom, I-ah-I wanna tell you about that bat..."

Lou's mom looked at him curiously.

"I- I think it belonged to someone famous... Lou Gehrig."

"The baseball player that went to your school?" she asked.

"Yeah."

"Well, why do you think that?"

"I found the bat at school, in the basement. The initials on the bat say LG," Lou's voice grew animated. "The bat is from the early 1900s. You can tell from the logo. The same time he was at my school."

His mom shook her head. "Do you know how many people have the initials LG?"

"Yeah, but it's gotta be his. I just feel it. I have Miss Sandy, the librarian, finding out if there were any other LGs at the school when Gehrig was there."

His mom shook her head again. "Well, if that really was

48

Lou Gehrig's bat, what are you doing playing with it? Maybe it's worth something. It should probably be in the Museum of Fame or something."

"Hall of Fame," Lou corrected.

"Whatever."

"I contacted a collector on the Internet, and he told me it could be worth $15,000."

His mom's eyes grew large. "Fifteen thousand dollars! Do you know how much money that is?!"

"I think so. Anyway, I just had to use it," Lou overlapped. "It… it gave me this… this feeling when I held it," he stammered. "It did something to me."

Lou's mom looked at her son like he was from outer space. "What are you talking about?"

"I *know* it was his bat. For the entire season I stunk. I only had three hits. When I use that bat… I'm unstoppable."

"Let me see this bat," his mother asked, curious and excited.

"All right." Lou ran out of the room and returned with the bat. He presented it to his mom.

She studied it carefully and smiled. "Lou, if this bat could be worth a lot of money, I don't want you to use it, okay? Use the bat I gave you for Christmas. That bat is *unbreakable*. When did you say you'd find out if this was his or not?"

"I don't know. Miss Sandy is helping me find out. There may not even be a way to prove it."

"Well, I don't want you using this bat. Understood?"

Lou's eyes swept the floor as he shook his head.

"Understood?" she repeated meaning serious business.

Lou let out a deep breath. "Yeah."

49

"Good." She paused. "Here." She handed him the bat. "It's very nice. It's also late. Let's get some sleep."

Lou took her book, put the bookmark inside and closed it. He then placed it on his mom's nightstand.

Lou's mom nodded a 'thank you.'

Lou tucked his mom in and kissed her forehead. He turned off her light. Lou then walked with the old, wooden Spalding on his shoulder to the front door and checked if it was locked. It was, so he headed for his room to sleep.

CHAPTER SIX
The Record

The tall wire fence that enclosed the all-dirt baseball field on the upper West Side of Manhattan was a small reminder to everyone that beyond their "field of dreams" was a busy, rough world. Life was difficult for the kids, coaches and parents on both teams—no different than for those playing and watching ball games on fields, parks and sandlots throughout the rest of the country. Lou looked at the fence as he and Daniel warmed up their arms by playing catch. He wished he had the ability to hit a ball over it. He also wished he had never told his mom about the bat. He had made up his mind the night before that he would try to continue his streak with the aluminum bat his mother had given him, just like she instructed. Sitting next to the metal Easton in his equipment bag, however, was the old, wooden Spalding, just for good luck. Lou had hoped maybe some of its power would rub off on the aluminum bat.

Then it happened—

"Lou, since you've been a real 'hitting machine' out there lately, I thought you'd be happy to know that I'm moving you up in the batting order." It was Coach Jeffer.

Lou tried to act enthused. "Ah, thanks, Coach."

Coach Jeffer patted Lou on the back and walked toward the bench.

"Hey! Gibson!" It was Bobby. "You nervous? This is a really big game. A win means a ticket to the playoffs. We're counting on that hot bat of yours to help us win."

Lou half-smiled. Bobby walked away. Lou motioned to Daniel that he was done playing catch.

Daniel ran up to him holding the ball. "What's wrong? You look terrible."

"Nothing." Lou took off his glove and walked toward the bench. He sat down and looked at his teammates. As they walked by him, each one slapped his hand. He felt accepted. *I don't want you using that bat.* His mother's words echoed inside his head.

"I saw the lineup card. Congratulations, Gibson! You made it to the heart of the batting order!" Bobby gave him a high-five. Lou nodded. Deep inside he longed for the security and feeling he knew the wooden Spalding would give him.

Coaches Jeffer and Tilly rallied the team on the bench. Each player stood up in a circle and placed their right hand in a circle, one on top of the other. All eyes stared at the joined hands in the center that united them. Lou looked up and glanced at his teammates. Like his, their eyes were filled with a blend of excitement and nervousness.

"Okay, Team. Go out there and play solid, fundamental baseball." Coach Jeffer stated.

"And win!" Coach Tilly added.

"Yeah, let's win this thing!" shouted Daniel, carried by the enthusiasm and feeling of brotherhood.

"Let's go, Indians! Teamwork!" everyone roared and broke the huddle.

"Big game, Lou. We'll be needing more hits from you, Kiddo," Coach Tilly put up his hand for a high five.

Lou slapped it half-heartedly. It was at that moment that Lou shut out hearing his mother's voice and decided to use the bat.

"Come on, Lou baby!" Coach Jeffer yelled.

"Yeah! Come on, Lou!" added the entire bench. Everyone stood excitedly on their feet. Fingers clenched the wire fence in front of them that protected them from foul balls.

"What inning is it? I lost track," asked Bobby, the Indians' third baseman.

"Bottom of the tenth," answered Calvin, the second baseman. He then quickly turned his attention back to the game. "Come on, Lou!"

Lou twirled his wooden Spalding bat, then held it above his shoulder and waited for the pitch, his stomach was all nerves. *Relax. Concentrate.* Suddenly, the tingling sensation in his hands and arms began to calm him. In came the pitch.

"Ball three!" the umpire yelled.

Frank Anderson, the Indians' catcher, stood anxiously on second base. He was the winning run. Calvin Welling stood on first. Frank nervously reminded himself of what he was supposed to do if the ball were hit to any player on the field.

Parents, siblings and other spectators watched from the bleachers. Their grips grew tighter and tighter upon hands, sweatshirts and anything in their possession.

Daniel watched his best friend from the on-deck circle. He desperately wanted to see him get a hit—a hit would bring in the winning run and take all the pressure off him.

It would also make Lou 6 for 6 for the day, giving him 11 consecutive hits! "Come on, Lou! You can do it! No pressure now!"

Lou glanced over his shoulder at Daniel as if to say "Yeah, right. No pressure."

"Come on, Lou!" one parent screamed.

"Lou! Lou! Lou!" the chants arose from the stands.

Lou felt a knot form in his stomach. He hesitated getting back into the batter's box. He looked into the stands and was glad his mom was not there watching. *She would kill me if she knew I was using the bat.* He watched the coach for a sign. None was given, only nervous and encouraging clapping. Lou wished he were more concerned with bringing in the winning run for his team. Instead, he was more concerned about getting another consecutive hit and the "fame" it would bring him. He knew with Gehrig's bat and the feeling it gave him that he could hit anything thrown by any pitcher. With that reminder, he dug his rear foot deep into the batter's box with confidence.

Those watching in the stands felt mixed emotions. It was late. Some wanted a hit so the team could win and finally go home. Others wanted to see the boy whom many thought should be playing chess instead of baseball keep the streak alive. The feelings caused some to raise their voices as if it were the World Series. Others stood in silence as if praying for a miracle.

As Lou raised the old, wooden Spalding above his shoulder, the noise from the crowd around him seemed to fade. In his mind it was silent, and he focused on the pitcher and the small white sphere that was about to be thrown.

The pitcher took his wind up and released the ball. Within seconds, hearts watching and cheering for both

54

sides skipped a beat as Lou swung wildly at a pitch that was way out of the strike zone.

The ball went sailing on a line drive right toward the third baseman, who leapt into the air and... came down empty handed.

Frank Anderson, heart racing, gazed up at Coach Jeffer as he headed for third. He instructed his legs to run harder as he saw the coach's arm waving him home. He hit third base with his right foot and ran as fast as he could while the left fielder threw the ball to the catcher.

Daniel watched the speed of the ball and the speed of his teammate intensely. "Down! Down!" he yelled.

Frank Anderson threw his pumping legs into a slide and a cloud of dust rose into the air as catcher, ball, foot and home plate touched each other simultaneously.

A second passed, then... "Safe!" bellowed the umpire.

Lou jumped up and down with delight as he stood a few feet off first base.

Coach Tilly ran up to him and gave him a high-five. "Lou, you're amazing! Great hit! We're headed for the playoffs!"

As Coach Jeffer and the rest of the team congratulated Frank at home plate, Lou suddenly noticed that his bat was being stepped on. His eyes widened with panic, and he sprinted toward home. "Hey! Hey!"

His teammates looked at him curiously as he speedily approached them with anger in his eyes. Lou aggressively pushed Doug Gillespie out of the way seconds after his cleat accidentally grazed Lou's bat. "Hey, my bat! Watch what you're doing!" Lou brushed everyone away, bent down and picked up his bat.

"What's your problem?" said Doug angrily as he regained his balance.

"You stepped on my bat! Try n' be more careful!" Lou wiped the dirt off the bat's barrel and handle with his batting glove. He held the bat closely as if it contained some remedy for heartache.

"It's just a piece of wood. You're bizarre, Gibson." Doug shook his head and regained his composure.

Lou watched his teammates, who didn't know if they should congratulate him for the winning hit and keeping the streak alive or reprimand him.

Just a piece of wood, Lou thought to himself sarcastically. *Hardly.*

The Indians shook the hands of their opponents—The Cubs—and then returned to their bench.

Coach Jeffer and Coach Tilly then gathered the team together for their usual discussion about the game. Coach Jeffer congratulated everyone for never giving up and for playing good, fundamental baseball.

Lou sat in between Daniel and Bobby, fidgeting, knowing that the discussion would soon turn to him.

Coach Jeffer adjusted his baseball cap. "You men really played like a team this evening. You hit the cutoff man. You hit behind runners when you were supposed to. You made all the big plays. This win was a team effort. I want to congratulate each and every one of you, but part of that team effort was a…"

Here it comes.

"… major individual accomplishment." Coach Jeffer paused. "Lou. I think we should give you a saliva test or something. What you've done with the bat these past two games is just remarkable."

"Tell me about it," said Doug Gillespie, almost under his breath. He looked at Lou as if to say "I stole your favorite line" and "I'm only joking… kinda."

56

Coach Jeffer read from the scorebook. "Lou Gibson...
four singles, two doubles, the game winning RBI, plus 3
other RBIs. You're 11 for 11, 11 hits in 11 at bats... that's
down right remarkable for a kid, who I have to admit, was-
n't hitting that well at the start of the season."

"It's a miracle," stated Bobby. The comment caused a
few agreeing chuckles.

Coach Jeffer held up the ball from the game's last hit.
"Lou, I don't think anyone would argue that you should
get the game ball." He tossed it to Lou. "Great job." He
started to clap. A few other players followed his lead and
clapped as well.

Lou caught the ball. His smile widened proudly.

"What you guys might not know or understand is what
Lou has done these past two games is quite a remarkable
accomplishment, even for a Big Leaguer. If Lou gets a hit
at his next at bat, he will tie the Major League record for
most consecutive hits. The record is 12 shared by Walt
Dropo in 1952 and Pinky Higgins in 1938."

"How do you know these things?" queried Bobby,
impressed.

Coach Jeffer grinned. "That's why I'm the coach."

Just then, everyone on both sides of the bench, to Lou's
left and right, stared at Lou. They saw him differently now
as if they were in the presence of greatness. Lou noticed
the expression on their faces and the look in their eyes—
and he liked it.

A moment of silence occurred, then... "I'm starving.
Can we go home now?" It was Daniel.

"Yes," proclaimed the coach. "Great game guys. Go
home, eat dinner and get a good night's sleep."

The team picked up their belongings, said their goodbyes and dispersed to their anxiously waiting parents, grandparents and rides.

Lou grabbed his bag and walked toward the field's exit.

"Hey, Lou! Gotta sec?" It was Coach Jeffer. He jogged up to him. "I want to talk to you."

"Yeah, Coach?" said Lou curiously.

"Listen, I mean this constructively. I know you were nervous during that last at bat, but you swung at a pitch that was *way* out of the strike zone. It would have been ball four and put you on first base. You…"

"I know," Lou overlapped. "But I swung at a ball so I wouldn't walk… on purpose. And I drilled it right over third base. It felt great."

"You also could have struck out on the next pitch if you missed that pitch swinging. That would have made two outs and…"

"But that didn't happen, did it?"

Coach Jeffer was taken aback. (It wasn't like Lou to interrupt him or anyone for that matter.) "No. It didn't. You were lucky."

"Luck had nothing to do with it."

Coach Jeffer nodded. "Lou, let's not get over-confident. I want every person on our team to get in the habit of swinging at good pitches only. You're one of my favorite kids…"

"But Coach, I got a hit."

"Walks are as good as a hit."

"But they're so boring."

Coach Jeffer didn't know what to say. This was the kid who used to be thankful for a walk. "Think about what I said, all right? I'll see ya next game, Lou." He turned to walk away.

Lou adjusted his equipment bag more comfortably over his shoulder. It was getting dark, and the breeze picked up like a thunderstorm was on its way. *Better get home. What a day! 11 for 11. One more hit to tie a Major League record. They'll be talking about it at school tomorrow for sure.*

Just then, Daniel ran up to Lou. "Hey… everything all right?" he asked, gesturing to the coach walking away.

"Yeah. You know coaches. They feel like they have to correct every little thing."

"Oh." Daniel paused as they started to walk. "Your mom couldn't make it either, huh?"

"No. She's working. Thank goodness."

"Mine, too." Daniel flung his equipment bag over his shoulder. "Hey, have you been taking private hitting lessons or something? This hitting streak is unbelievable."

Should I tell him now?

"To be honest, I never knew you had it in you." He paused as they approached the opening in the fence that led to the street. "Do ya think you could take a look at my swing and give me some tips?"

Lou stopped in his tracks and studied Daniel. *Can I trust him? He never told anyone I liked Stephanie Kalez last year.*

"What? Why are you looking at me like that?"

Lou smiled. "Listen, there's been something I've been *dying* to tell you. I'd love to give you some hitting tips, but I'm not so sure they'd help."

Daniel's face suddenly took on a confused expression.

"Here. Look." Lou unzipped his equipment bag and took out the wooden Spalding bat. "Check this out." He showed Daniel the initials on the bottom of the bat.

"Yeah, so?" said Daniel reading the two carved letters. "That's your initials."

"I know they're mine," replied Lou sarcastically. He wanted to knock on Daniel's forehead like he was knocking on a door. "They're also somebody else's."

Daniel entered deep thought. "Yeah. Lots of people have the initials LG in this world. I'm not getting it."

"No dah." Lou shook his head. "Think. Who is the most famous graduate from our school?"

Daniel reflected then- "Lou Gehrig."

Lou raised his eyebrows and waited.

Daniel was silent for a long moment. Suddenly, a look of disbelief formed on his face. "You mean…"

"That's right. I think this was his bat."

Daniel dropped his bag. "Let me see that again." He quickly reached for the bat.

Lou pulled it back. "Hey, easy. Be gentle, and I'll let you hold it."

Daniel carefully took hold of the bat. He rocked it like he was starting his hitting stance. "Wooden bats feel so different than aluminum." He took a swing. "I don't know if it's because its wood or what, but this bat feels… special."

"Are your hands tingling?"

"No. Why?"

"Never mind."

"How do you know it's his? Where'd you get it? Why are you playing with it? If this is his, it could be worth something," Daniel blurted. "Man, if this is his bat, that would be *so* cool. I don't know if I'd be using it if I were you."

"I *have* to use it. That's why I don't think I can give you much advice with your swing."

"What? You think it's magical or something?"

"Magical? I don't know. All I know is that at the beginning of the season I couldn't hit a beach ball if it were thrown at me. Now, I'm unstoppable." He paused for a moment reflecting. "You have to promise me you won't tell anyone about this." Lou looked Daniel straight in the eye. "This is serious. No one can know."

"I won't tell anyone. I promise." Daniel took an imaginary key and locked his lips, then threw the key away. "It's in the vault."

"Good. Thanks." Lou stuck out his hand to seal the agreement. "Not a soul?"

"Not a soul."

They shook hands.

CHAPTER SEVEN
The Batter's Box

The story about Lou's accomplishment spread like wild fire throughout PS 132. It started with the sixth grade and worked its way down to the first. Kids who never heard of Lou Gibson before now knew his name. Others who never liked him before now claimed him as a friend. Through e-mail and "the grapevine," teachers and students alike all talked about Lou for days. Many wouldn't believe that the boy who couldn't control his laughter in class or get a drink of water from the water fountain without dribbling it all over himself could control a baseball bat and consistently hit a ball. Some marveled at the change; some didn't care. Either way it was the main topic of conversation.

Lou reveled in the attention as he watched his reputation stock climb to a level that would make any Wall Street executive wish they could invest in him. Mrs. Troast called him "The Pride of PS 132." The biggest sign of popularity came, however, when Lizandra Collins personally invited him to her birthday party. She had never paid much attention to Lou before, and now she flirted with him like he was a rising movie star. Lou was now part of the "cool" crowd, and he loved it.

Justin didn't believe a word of it until every kid on Lou's team told him it was true. He still waved it off with his hand as a freak accident and luck. Justin wished he were facing Lou in the next game so he could ensure that Lou's hitting streak would end, but that was not on the schedule.

Even with all the newfound attention, Lou still made time to try and accomplish his #1 mission. He approached Miss Sandy so many times asking her if she found out anything yet that he was on the verge of becoming annoying. Miss Sandy's research revealed that the records on past students were still on file. The files were kept in the school's annex building, and she hadn't had time to get there yet. She could see the impatience mounting in Lou's eyes, so she made a promise to go there soon.

One additional question remained for Lou and the rest of the kids at school—Would he tie or break the consecutive hit record?

The first playoff game for the Indians matched the team against the Orioles. The battle took place at the same field as the last game. This time the metal bleachers were entirely full. An overflow of people stood and watched from around the perimeter of the field. The playoffs brought in more family members and friends, and because of news of "The Streak," this game had more fans watching it than usual.

During the pre-game practice, players on the Indians debated over whether it was better to use wood or aluminum bats. Everyone decided that even though Lou's streak was happening with the use of a wooden bat, that aluminum bat's "ruled." No way would anyone ever use a wooden bat—until they made it to the pros.

Lou laughed silently to himself at the conclusion, but when Frank Anderson asked if he could use Lou's bat, his laughter stopped. His eyes widened, and he responded with a definite "No way!" It was not to be argued and everyone on the team heard it and understood.

The game started. During the first inning, players on both sides were nervous. However, as his turn in the batting rotation approached, not a soul on the field was more nervous than Lou.

I can't do this. This is way too much pressure. Lou couldn't focus on a word Coach Jeffer said. Butterflies were bouncing like ping-pong balls off the walls of his stomach. His hands trembled. He looked into the stands for his mom. *Good. She's not here yet.*

"Take a deep breath and relax. What you've accomplished is already outstanding." Coach Jeffer had his hands placed on Lou's shoulders, and the two stared at each other like they were about to fight a war. "You don't have to tie this record, Lou. It doesn't matter. I wish I never even mentioned it."

"Tell me about it."

"Just get in there and do your best. Hit or miss, I still believe in you. No matter what, you're a great kid."

A smile jumped from Coach Jeffer's face to Lou.

"Remember, just relax."

Lou took a deep breath, the deepest he ever took in his life, and turned around. As he slowly walked from the third base coach's box toward home plate, people were chanting his name. His helmet, which was a little too big, joggled left and right. Lou adjusted it with his left hand while the

Spalding rested on his right shoulder. *Just relax. This doesn't matter.*

Daniel picked out his bat from the selection near the bench. He watched Lou walk toward home. Their friendship had started in kindergarten. They both played Tee ball together in the first grade. He wanted to see his friend do well. As he imagined himself in Lou's shoes, his stomach began to tighten.

"This is intense, actually 'incredible' is a better word." It was Bobby, who always sat near the bats. "I hope he strikes out so we can get this over with."

Daniel didn't say a word.

Lou was about to lead off the second inning. He approached the batter's box and glanced at the pitcher who leered back at him. The boy on the mound looked like a bull getting ready to ram a bullfighter. It was obvious this was not going to be a free ticket to first base.

I can't delay this anymore. Just do it. Lou dug his rear foot into the left side of the batter's box. *Let's get this over with.* Lou's heart was beating like a rabbit, and his palms were sweaty. He tuned out the crowd chanting his name and the infield calling him a "whiffer."

"If he gets a hit, it will be a miracle. This streak is down right incredible," declared Bobby.

"You'd get a hit every time, too, if you had Lou Gehrig's bat." Daniel's heart skipped as he realized what had come out of his mouth.

"What?" Bobby didn't understand.

The pitcher started his wind up.

Both boys focused their attention on Lou.

In came the pitch. It was going to be a strike. Lou launched his swing and-

WHACK!

The ball hit the bat right in the sweet spot and sailed toward right field.

Silence fell across the park. Mouths dropped wide open as all eyes watched the small white pearl with red laces fly up, up, up and OVER the fence!

"There's nothing so beautiful as the sound of a baseball hitting a wooden bat!" proclaimed Coach Tilly, with complete and utter joy.

Grin after grin formed and leapt from face to face throughout the park, except of course on the faces of the Oriole players. Shouts of joy and applause filled the air.

Lou wore the biggest grin. He beamed with pride as he jogged toward first base. It was his very first home run, and he tried to mimic the home run trot of a Major Leaguer. Although he felt like he was trotting too fast, he couldn't help himself. It was as if he were asleep and in a dream. He waited for something to jolt him awake and to find himself suddenly in his bed. As he rounded third base and was hit on the behind by Coach Jeffer, he realized that this was really happening.

Waiting for him at home plate were his teammates. They clapped and jumped up and down with excitement.

Lou stopped one step before reaching home base, then stamped on it. Just then, everyone jumped on top of him, patted him on the back and gave him a "high-five." Lou felt like he was being mugged, but loved every second of it. He looked in the crowd for his mom. Part of him wished she could be there to watch his finest moment. Another part of him was relieved she was not there.

Coach Jeffer caught himself wearing a broad smile. He laughed as the tension left his body. He watched his "men" surround and congratulate their teammate and felt deep inside like he had made a difference. Each boy was special to him, but none more so than Lou. Coach Jeffer called a timeout and motioned for Lou to meet him half way. "Hey," greeted the Coach as he jogged up to Lou.

"Hey." Lou was a bit out of breath and overwhelmed.

"Way to go, Lou. I'm proud of you." Coach Jeffer put his arm around Lou.

"Thanks," replied Lou. " This is awesome. Now, I just gotta break it. Honestly… I'm proud of me, too."

"I bet. You enjoy it."

"I bet you wish I could bat for the entire team," Lou stated.

Coach Jeffer stood erect, not liking the statement or the attitude behind it. "Let's not get over-confident, okay?"

"Why not? I've been *the best* lately…"

Coach Jeffer stared at Lou. An awkward moment passed; then, Lou turned on his heels and ran back towards the bench. As he walked past the bats, he saw that his mom had arrived and was being informed by everyone in the stands about what had just transpired. Their eyes met, and she smiled at him proudly as people were still talking to her. Lou waved, then sat down on the bench where everyone congratulated him some more.

As the players on the field got ready for the next Indian batter, Coach Jeffer could not help but feel haunted by Lou's comment.

"I gotta tell you… *You* are awesome. I'm impressed," admitted Frank. The two boys hit fists.

Lou smiled at Frank, then focused on the game as the next pitch was about to be thrown. Suddenly, his jaw dropped and his eyes widened in horror, his face a contorted mask of amazement and alarm. Mounted just above

Daniel Eng's right shoulder was the old, wooden Spalding bat. *Oh my...*

Before Lou could scream a word, the pitch came in. He felt his world turn from real time into slow motion as he watched Daniel swing and make contact with the ball.

Everyone winced at the sound. The ball slowly rose into the air and was caught by the third baseman.

As Daniel ran to first base, Lou jolted toward the field and his bat.

Lou's mom anxiously watched her son run onto the field.

The sound the bat made when it hit the ball echoed through Lou's mind as if he were in a nightmare. As he slowed from his frantic sprint, his heart sank as he picked up his precious bat and saw that it was cracked.

Disbelief filled his entire being. He longed to wake up, but knew he wasn't asleep. His blood pumped vigorously through his veins, and his knuckles grew white as he clenched the bat in his two hands. Slowly he looked up to find the source of his pain.

Daniel had already reached first base and knew he was out. Fear had filled his body with each step he had taken toward the base. From the moment he made contact with the ball, he knew that the bat was cracked—and that he was in trouble. He watched Lou holding his bat as if it were a dying friend. Suddenly, their eyes met. If looks could kill, Daniel knew he would be history. The quickest way back to the bench would take Daniel right toward Lou. He didn't know what to do.

Lou knelt on the ground. With the bat in his hands, he leered at Daniel. Each breath he took punctuated a more angry thought.

Lou's mom watched her son holding the bat and figured out what had happened. She moved herself through the crowd and ran down the stands to the fence.

"What's going on?" Coach Tilly asked Daniel, as he stood in the first base coach's area.

"Oh, man. This is not good," observed Doug Gillespie.

Everyone on the bench jumped to his feet.

"You idiot! You jerk!" yelled Lou fiercely. "I can't believe this! You idiot! What were you thinking?" Lou screamed as if a cork had just been let out of his mouth.

Daniel didn't know what to say or which way to walk. "I'm sorry."

"I *never* said you could use my bat!"

The entire infield curiously gazed at each other as if to say, "What's going on?"

"Time!" bellowed the umpire, not understanding what was happening.

Coach Jeffer jogged toward Lou.

"Lou, calm down," Coach Tilly suggested. "What's the big deal?"

Players on both teams approached the field closer to listen.

"That jerk broke my bat!" Lou was irate, on the verge of hostility.

"Calm down. I'll buy you a new one," offered Coach Jeffer, trying to restore peace.

"You can't replace *this* bat!" Lou yelled at Coach Jeffer as if he were reprimanding a child.

Lou's mom watched from behind the fence that separated the spectators from the field. She wanted to run out onto the field, but realized she shouldn't.

"It's just a wooden bat. I'll get you one just like it. I

70

promise." Coach Jeffer felt like he was negotiating with a two-year-old having a temper tantrum.

"You can't! You don't understand…"

Bobby listened. His eyes widened with sudden understanding. "I think I get it…. It's Lou Gehrig's bat." He stated it like a detective who just solved a mystery.

Lou shot a piercing look at Daniel. "You told him? I don't believe you!" He rushed toward Daniel like he was going to tackle him.

Coach Tilly quickly stepped in front, blocked him and wrapped his arm around him.

"Let me go!" Lou held onto the bat with one hand and tried to pry the coach's hand off with the other.

"Gibson! Calm yourself and get your behind back to our bench right now!" Coach Jeffer ordered. He pointed toward the bench. His eyes meant business.

"We have a game to play, gentlemen," interrupted the umpire impatiently. "Get your players under control."

The Indians had all gathered behind the backstop.

Coach Jeffer gave Lou a stern look.

Lou stopped his pursuit and Coach Tilly gently released him.

Lou was still fuming, but he allowed Coach Jeffer to escort him back to the bench.

Daniel cautiously followed.

"All right, now! Let's play ball!" the umpire called. He tossed a ball to the pitcher and a new batter, Calvin Welling, entered the batter's box.

Lou's mom now stood behind the fence near the Indian's bench.

As Lou walked by, he noticed her out of the corner of his eye, but refused to make eye contact with her.

"Why is that bat even here?!" she yelled.

Lou didn't respond as Coach Jeffer silently escorted him to the bench. Daniel followed.

Daniel Eng! Do you know how much that bat might be worth? Lou's mom wanted to yell the words at the top of her lungs, but refrained.

Coach Jeffer shook his head and took his position back in the third base coach's box.

Daniel sat down sheepishly at the other end, a safe distance away. He looked down at Lou who huffed in anger, his hands and eyes fixed on his cracked bat.

Frank approached Lou and smiled. "Hey, was that really Lou Gehrig's bat? Can I see it?" He reached for the cracked wooden club.

"Get away from me!" Lou hollered, as he brushed Frank's hand away. He let out a steamy huff then darted his eyes at Daniel.

Daniel didn't know what to do. He looked away and sat with his head held low.

The game continued around them, but neither cared.

Daniel slowly approached Lou, who noticed him out of the corner of his eye. "Listen, I'm sorry. I…"

Lou slowly gazed at Daniel through two piercing eyes. "Get. Away. From. Me." Each syllable delivered a verbal punch.

Daniel paused, then- "I'm *really* sorry."

Lou sprang to his feet and shoved Daniel hard. "I said 'Get away from me.'"

"Calm down, man!" ordered Bobby as he put his arm between the two boys.

"Gibson! Cool it NOW!" It was Coach Jeffer. "I don't want to say it again!"

Lou turned and walked to the end of the bench where he sat down alone.

His teammates tried the best they could to ignore him. Some of the bigger kids whispered quiet comments like "Loser" as they walked by him. Everyone else tried to focus on the game.

Lou's mom still steamed angrily as she paced back and forth behind the fence.

Competition returned to order. Coach Jeffer reminded everyone that they were in a playoff game and that a loss would end their season.

Daniel and Lou kept a large distance between them as they ran on and off the field and while they were on the bench.

Two innings later, Lou's next turn at bat came. His metal Easton brought him no tingling sensation, goose bumps or hits. Consumed with anger, Lou struck out. The streak was over. Lou couldn't believe how his life changed so quickly in just a few innings. Just moments ago, it seemed, he stood on top of the world. He hit a home run, and he tied a Major League record. It was indeed his life's greatest moment. Now, he should've been holding his wooden Spalding and have broken the record. There should be cheers, accolades and applause... There should be that sweet feeling of success beating inside his breast. Instead, there was silence throughout the park. Those who wanted to see the record broken were disappointed. Those upset by his strange reaction to his bat being broken earlier were glad to see him fail. No expletive came out of Lou's mouth. As he walked away from the plate, he took his unbreakable metal bat and flung it against the fence.

Coach Jeffer shook his head in disappointment.

Lou stood with slumped shoulders, then walked past Daniel, who was approaching home plate. He bumped

Daniel's shoulder with his own. "This friendship is history, Jerk." He walked back to his spot on the bench. Not a word was said by anyone, and he didn't care.

CHAPTER EIGHT
Errors

Lou had run ahead of his mom the whole way home, then locked himself in his room. Not since Lou's dad passed away one year earlier had the Gibson home been so emotional.

"Lou. Open this door. We need to talk! Now!" his mom ordered.

"No way! Go away!" Lou replied as he lay on his bed. Lou replayed the evening's events over and over again in his head. He saw himself hitting the ball over the fence for a homerun and trotting around the bases. He remembered the look of joy on his teammate's faces when he crossed home plate.

Lou then replayed Daniel's swing. He could still hear that fatal blow and his bat go "crack!" *I can't believe he did that. He's ruined everything.* Lou took off his Indians jersey and put on a tee shirt.

There was banging on the door. "Let me in there, NOW! Understand!"

"No way!" Lou opened his baseball bag and gingerly

took out the old Spalding. The bat was still in one piece, but it had a nice split just above the handle. As he stared at the crack, he envisioned in his mind each and every hit he got with the bat. Swing after swing played like a Lou Gibson highlight reel on the screen of his brain. *I was awesome with this thing.* Lou noticed the tingling sensation was now gone. It was as if the crack had leaked all of the bat's power.

Lou studied the crack some more and wondered whether or not it could be fixed. The idea made him leap to his feet and turn on his computer. In a matter of moments, Lou searched the Internet for information on bat repair. A spark of hope ignited within him! As quickly as the hope came, though, it faded. There in front of him, was a web site on baseball bats with a section called "Bat Repair." The fourth paragraph stated that wooden bats could indeed be repaired and restored, but only for display purposes. They would still not be durable enough for everyday play. We can put a man on the moon, but we can't fix a bat, thought Lou.

Suddenly, there was a noise coming from his door. It sounded like his mom was trying to take the door lock apart with a screwdriver. "Open this door, Lou!"

"No! Not now!" With hope extinguished, Lou began to feel angry again. He reminded himself of the two lousy strikeouts he had during his last two at bats. Even though his team won by a score of 5 to 4, they didn't do so with the help of his "hot" bat. It seemed things were just the way they were before the vintage wooden Spalding baseball bat entered his life. *I'd be better off if I had never found this thing.* Lou put the bat in the corner of his room. Whether the bat once belonged to Henry Louis Gehrig or not really didn't matter to him right now.

"This is the last time! If you don't open this door, I'll get the Super, and he'll open it!" Lou's mom bellowed. Her voice was even more serious.

Lou cautiously opened the door.

His mom burst through. "Who do you think you are locking me out?! Don't you ever do that again, hear me?" She stared at Lou. "Do you hear me?"

"Yes, ma'am," Lou replied, his head held low.

"What's gotten into you? Tell me… Why was that bat at that game?! Do you know what that could have meant to us?"

Lou didn't answer.

"You know, I've been angry, upset and even frustrated with you… There are times I don't understand you and just wish you'd listen…" Her voice cracked full of emotion.

Lou stared at the floor.

"But tonight… Tonight was the first time I was disappointed in you… What were you thinking? Why was that bat at that game?"

Lou looked up and stared at her. He didn't know how to answer.

"If that bat did belong to that Gehrig guy, don't you know it could solve our problems. You read the papers; you watch the news; you know more than I that all that sports memorabilia stuff is hot. I'm working day and night and that…"

Lou sat silently.

Lou's mom interrupted herself. "Well, I'll tell you one thing… that Daniel Eng is not welcome around here anymore. You got that?"

"He knew it was Gehrig's bat… or might be. He knew I didn't want anyone to use it." Lou blurted.

"What he did was wrong, but so was what you did. I

77

can't believe you didn't listen to me. This whole thing could have been avoided, if only you had listened to me." She paused. "So, tell me… what was that bat doing at that game, when I told you *not* to use it?"

Lou sat frozen like a statue looking at the ground.

"It didn't walk there on its own," his mom continued.

Lou raised his head and swallowed a lump in his throat. "I brought it to the game," he confessed softly. "I used it… but *I* didn't crack it…"

Lou's mom shook her head. "No kidding. What in the…" she stopped herself. "What were you thinking? Louis Michael Gibson… I did not raise a stupid boy…"

"I- I wasn't thinking," he overlapped.

She shook her head faster, exasperated. "I- I- don't know *what* to say. I'm so mad at you I can't even think straight. You… Oh! Just go to bed! The damage is done. I- I having nothing else to say. Except that you're grounded."

Lou's eyes widened, but he didn't argue.

"We'll talk more about this tomorrow, but consider yourself a prisoner of this house. I hope you learned something from this…" She turned around and headed for the door, then pointed her finger. "I'm serious. Daniel's not welcome anymore in this home."

Lou nodded. "I don't think you have to worry about that," he replied softly.

CHAPTER NINE
In a Pickle

News about the prior day's events quickly spread through the PS 132 grapevine. The next day everyone at school talked about Lou. First, about his act of tying the Major League record for consecutive hits with a towering homerun, then about the bat cracking and the fight with Daniel. The conversation switched to the fact that the bat might have belonged to Gehrig and that Lou was playing like his old self again. It was material for tabloid headlines, and like most people the kids at PS 132 ate up the gossipy stories and passed them along one by one.

Lou knew everyone was talking about him. He wished that things could have been different—that they could have talked about him breaking the record and about how great he was. *Man, yesterday I was a star, today, a…* Lou shuddered at the thought.

Justin Rivers took the bull by the horns and told Lou that his hitting streak was a "freak" of luck. He promised he would strike Lou out if they ever faced each other in a game. Justin then gave Lou the nickname "Freakazoid."

The name stuck and when Lou walked down the halls, more than a just a few gutsy boys who were bigger called him the name. It was Lou's ultimate test of self-control. Each time he heard the name, he wanted to take every ounce of energy he had and channel it into a tackle or punch. Although the anger built up inside, Lou controlled it by thinking hard and didn't let it result in action.

This didn't make things any easier for Daniel, who tried to reconcile the friendship. The night before, he called Lou at home. Lou's mom yelled at him again and wouldn't let him speak to her son. Daniel sent Lou e-mails. Lou deleted them, unread.

Earlier, Daniel approached Lou in homeroom. Lou ignored him. He tried to talk to him in the hallway. Lou brushed him off. He left an apology note in his desk. Lou ripped it up, unread. Lou blamed Daniel for the entire mess and wanted no part of him. *If the bat were still in one piece, even if I didn't break the record, things wouldn't be this bad.*

As Lou sat in Mrs. Troast's history class, he surveyed his classmates in the room. It seemed those who were his new friends yesterday now ignored him. His stock had tumbled like he was caught up in a sudden stock market crash. Lou caught the eye of Lizandra. She immediately turned away. Moments before class Lizandra had uninvited him to her birthday party. *Can it get any worse?*

Suddenly, there was a knock on the classroom door. A student entered with a note for Mrs. Troast. She read it silently, then looked up.

"Mr. Gibson… the Principal would like to see you."

"Oooooooooooooooooooowwwwww," the kids in the class chimed in unison, sounding like a chorus of owls.

Lou stood up and walked toward the door.

"Freakazoid," whispered Andre Robinson so Lou could hear.

Lou did his best to ignore Andre and approached Mrs. Troast. He searched her eyes for any sign if she knew what this was about and if she would tell him.

Mrs. Troast simply shrugged her shoulders and gave Lou a reassuring smile that no matter what, everything should be all right.

Lou lethargically stepped into the hallway. The door slowly closed behind him. He could hear some laughter coming from behind the door and Mrs. Troast reprimanding the class. Yeah, this is really funny, he thought sarcastically. He aimed himself in the direction of the school's office. *What did I do now?* Even Mrs. Troast's warm, gentle smile couldn't settle his nerves. He thought back to every moment of school that day and couldn't think of anything he had done wrong. *Oh, no. What if something happened to Mom?* He quickened his pace as a feeling of fear overcame him.

"Hello, Mr. Gibson." It was Mr. Townson, the principal. He was dressed in an old brown suit. He scratched his head of curly, balding brown hair, as Lou entered his office. Mr. Townson said nothing as he seated himself behind his desk and motioned for Lou to sit as well.

Lou adjusted himself in his seat, which was much lower than Mr. Townson's chair. Hanging on the wall in front of him were two photographs—one was of the old Yankee Stadium, and the other was an action shot of Lou Gehrig taking a powerful swing. There was a long moment of silence, then-

"I hear a rumor that you may have found a bat

belonging to Lou Gehrig… is that true?" asked Mr. Townson, with a bit of powder sugar from a donut frosting his bushy mustache.

Lou sighed in relief, knowing this conversation was not going to be about his mom. "Uh, yeah."

"The rumor also says that you found this bat on school property… is that true?" Mr. Townson folded his arms and leaned forward on his desk with eager interest.

"Yeah."

Mr. Townson stood up, walked around his desk and looked out his office window. His back faced Lou. "Mr. Gibson, I don't think I have to remind you that anything found on school property should belong to the school."

Oh, no. Lou's heart skipped a beat. "But Mr. Broom gave it to me," Lou's voice pleaded.

Principal Townson turned around. "I'll have a talk with Mr. Broom about that." He hesitated. "Lou, didn't it ever cross your mind that the school should have that bat?"

"No. I didn't know it was Gehrig's bat when Mr. Broom gave it to me. It was just an old bat. I still don't even know if it was his… Besides, it belonged to someone with the initials LG, not the school."

The expression on Mr. Townson' face turned serious. "Don't you think that if it is Lou Gehrig's bat that the school should have it?"

Lou didn't answer.

"I'm requesting that you return the bat to the school…"

Lou's eyes and mouth widened.

"If you like, I can talk to your parents about this?"

Lou sat in silence. Mr. Townson's eyes seemed to penetrate his conscience. He sighed, then- "Um. No, sir. That's all right. I'll… I'll give it back." Lou wished he could talk to

82

a lawyer or someone who knew what was right. The bat, which originally brought great joy, was now bringing trouble. *Maybe it's best if I don't have it, after all.*

That afternoon Lou went home and got the bat. His mom was at work, so he made up his mind that he wasn't going to tell her about what had happened. "Maybe this is for the best," he kept telling himself.

Tears ran down his face as he wrapped the wooden Spalding in some old, brown paper shopping bags. He escorted it back to school where he presented it to Mr. Townson. A wisp of a smile formed on Mr. Townson's face as he took hold of the bat. He thanked Lou and reminded him that he did the right thing. Lou walked home and didn't know what to think or feel. "If I did the right thing, then why do I feel so bad," Lou asked himself.

The traffic up and down the aisles of Lombardi's grocery store was extremely busy. Lou handed his mom bottles of salsa and she stocked the shelves. (This was part of Lou's punishment for disobeying his mother.)

"This isn't so much fun, is it?" Lou's mom asked.

Lou made a face, which told his mom he agreed. He looked down the aisle and saw an unwelcome sight— Daniel and his mother pushing their grocery cart directly towards them. Lou handed his mother another jar of salsa and turned his back towards them.

"Well, hello. If it isn't Mr. Baseball." It was Lou's mom. She was addressing Daniel. Her tone was sarcastic. "Hello, Nancy," she added politely to Daniel's mother.

"Hi, Dolores. How are you?" Nancy Eng asked without a clue as to what had happened. She was slender with bony shoulders. Her black hair was lined with some streaks of gray.

Lou and Daniel exchanged awkward glances.

"I've been better."

A look of concern appeared on Lou's face.

"I thought you usually work the check out?" Mrs. Eng asked, trying to make conversation. Her eyes were brown and expressed sincere interest.

"Our stock boy called in sick again, and I thought this was something Lou and I could do together," Lou's mom replied. "Its part of his punishment."

Embarrassed, Lou looked down at his sneakers.

"Maybe Daniel would like to help him?" Lou's mom added, looking into his eyes.

A look of concern appeared on Daniel's face.

"Daniel's always willing to help a friend," replied Mrs. Eng, feeling some tension in the air.

"You didn't tell your mom, did you?" Lou's mom asked Daniel.

"Mom…" Lou started to speak, but was cut off.

"Tell me what?" Mrs. Eng questioned.

"Well, it seems that your son decided to use my son's bat and broke it. Turns out it could be a very expensive, one of a kind, bat…"

"If Daniel broke something, we'll be happy to replace it," Mrs. Eng overlapped, as she searched her son's eyes for an explanation.

"Oh, good. Because we think it's worth several thousand dollars. We'll bill you." Lou's mom finished her sentence. Her words caused Mrs. Eng to double take.

"Daniel, you never… Is this true?"

Daniel tilted his head down. "Kinda," he replied.

"Kinda!" Lou's mom raised her voice causing other shoppers to look at them. She paused and softened her tone. "How dare you say 'Kinda'. And how dare you keep what you did from your mother." She paused and shook her head as she placed a jar of salsa on the shelf.

Lou's face turned red with embarrassment.

"Dolores, I apologize for anything my son may have done."

Lou's mom was silent on purpose. By this time, others had gathered around, including the Store Manager, and were watching.

"Well…" Mrs. Eng huffed. "If we owe you anything, I'll make sure you get paid back. The Eng family always rights their wrongs. And we do so without being rude. I guess you never learned that one in church." Punctuating her comment, Mrs. Eng stared at the cross around Dolores Gibson's neck. She then put her arm around Daniel and they walked away.

Lou's mom looked down at her chest to see what Mrs. Eng was staring at. She then looked up and noticed everyone staring at her. It was, however, the look of disappointment in Lou's eyes that got to her the most.

The sky was overcast with heavy, sullen clouds. It was a dark evening for baseball—and for Lou. The second play-off game placed the Indians against the Giants, Tanya Sanchez's team. Though it looked like it could rain at any moment, both teams decided it best to try their luck and get the game in. All the boys had a good time making fun of the fact that the Giants had a girl on their team. However, their comments were soon put to rest, and to shame, when Tanya herself responded with the fact that her batting average was .420—the highest in the League. "What are you batting?" she asked. From that second on, no one said a word.

Lou and Daniel avoided each other from the moment they saw one another.

Coach Jeffer watched them and shook his head.

The game started and it was immediately a fierce battle. Tanya Sanchez, the Giants lead off batter, hit a double down the right field line. Tanya later scored on a base hit. The Giants gained two more runs the same inning.

The next inning the Indians rallied back and Daniel managed to hit a line drive over the pitcher's head.

Inning by inning, the lead switched from team to team. Lou, however, made no contribution to the hit or run quotient. At the end of five innings, he was 0 for 3 with two strikeouts and a ground out, which made him 0 for 5 consecutively. He plopped himself on the bench and buried his head in his hands.

"Dude, slumps are all mental." It was Bobby. He placed his hand on Lou's shoulder like a sage. "The more you think about it the worse it gets. Focus on your mechanics. You're pulling your head out and swinging wildly at almost everything. It's not easy hitting a round object with another round object."

Lou squinted at Bobby, surprised he was even talking to him.

"As a hitter, you have a choice of what to think about." Bobby's tone was serious. "Think about successful at bats and proper mechanics. You did it before. You can do it again," he said with friendly encouragement. "Don't think about the slump." Bobby started to walk away, then turned. "It's a game of averages... just don't think about yours cause its lower than an ant's belly." He laughed. "I'm only joking…"

Lou laughed. It was not a pleasant, hearty laugh, but ever so much better than none.

The game moved at a furious pace. The eighth inning came faster than anyone could have imagined. The score was tied. The rain had managed to hold off; however, its threat added more tension to everyone playing and watching.

As Lou waited for his turn at bat in the on-deck circle, he tried to focus on everything Bobby had said.

The Giant's pitcher had walked two batters, putting the winning run at second.

Lou wiped the dirt off his Easton and tried to block all thoughts of his Spalding, Principal Townson, Daniel and everything else out of his mind.

"Time!" It was Coach Jeffer.

Lou wondered what was wrong.

"Gillespie! Pick up a bat! You're pinch hitting!"

Doug Gillespie jumped from his seat. He nervously and excitedly searched for his club among the bats.

Lou's mouth was open and he gazed at the Coach with glassy eyes.

Coach Jeffer jogged up to Lou as he walked dejectedly toward the bench. "Lou, sorry, but I had to do it. It's for the good of the team. I need a right hander in there and you…" Coach Jeffer looked over at Doug who was waiting for instruction.

"And I stink. Is that what you were going to say?" Lou muttered.

"No. This isn't the time. We can talk about this later." Coach Jeffer turned and focused his attention on Doug. "Come on, Doug! Relax and be a hitter in there!"

As Lou walked slowly back to the bench, he could feel his teammates agreeing with the coach's decision. He dragged his bat behind him and looked up at the faces in the bleachers watching the game. He noticed how many of the player's fathers were there. He wondered if things would be different if his dad were around.

The Gibson home was once again quiet. As Lou took off his Indians jersey and threw it in his laundry basket, he could not help but feel envious and jealous of Doug. His team was now headed for the championship thanks to him. "All that applause and cheering could have been mine," Lou thought. *If I only had...* Lou looked in the corner of his room, the spot where he had kept the Spalding. *Somehow, that spot will always seem empty now.*

Lou sat on his bed and took off his sneakers. *God... How did all this happen? I don't have the bat. I don't have any friends. I have nothing. Why am I being punished?* Just then, his mom lightly tapped on the door and came in.

"Mom, not now," Lou growled.

"Sorry. I have to talk to you." There were tears in her eyes.

Lou wondered if someone had died or what could have caused her tears.

Lou's mom sighed. She sat down beside him on the bed. She looked even more tired than usual. "Honey, I... I was wrong."

Lou's head twitched as he looked her in the eye. She had never before said she was wrong to him.

"I've been thinking about your father. And what I did was so wrong."

A curious look formed on Lou's face.

88

"I should never have reacted the way I did. Here I am trying to teach you about self control and I didn't even do it myself. I should never have confronted Daniel and his mom. I shouldn't have said a word. I should have just let my anger go. That's what your father would have done."

"Really?"

Lou's mom scratched her face. "Oh, your father would have gotten mad, but he never would have said the things I said. I'm always so bad with these things… I was wrong to be angry with Daniel. I should've never yelled at him on the phone or confronted them at the store. And I should never have told you he isn't welcome in our home…"

Lou opened his mouth to speak…

His mother cut him off. "You know, one time… well, one time, I broke your daddy's watch. I didn't mean to do it. I dropped it while I was playfully trying to put it on him in the park one day. And it fell on cement. The crystal cracked and the watch stopped ticking."

"Did he get mad?" Lou asked.

"Did he ever. It was his grandfather's watch. His father had given it to him, and he planned to give it to you someday."

"Really? Where is it?"

"It's in our safe deposit box. You'll get it when you graduate from high school. That was your father's wish. Anyhow, your father was furious with me. He didn't speak to me for hours, but he forgave me. It cost over $150 dollars to have the crystal replaced and the watch fixed… I felt so bad, but your daddy told me that he loved me more than that old watch." She wiped a tear from her eye. "Your daddy was a good man. I miss him. Lord knows I need him so."

Lou put his arm around her waist and embraced her.

His mom hugged him hard, then stroked his face with her fingers. "I asked myself, 'What if you had cracked the bat?' I still would have been mad, but I would have forgiven you. It's just a hunk of wood after all. It may be a valuable piece of wood, but still…"

Lou stared at his mom. They hadn't talked about his dad in a long time, and he liked the way it made him feel.

Lou's mom smiled reflectively. "You know, your father wasn't perfect, but he always tried to give God the glory in the good times and the bad." She chuckled, "He used to say, 'I can take the good with the bad.' He said that because he had faith. We need to be more like that. I saw that bat as a ticket to make things easier for us. I guess I'm so tired of being tired lately I can't even think straight. With or without that bat, God will provide. That's what I felt your father would have told me."

Dolores Gibson studied her son. She knew him better than anyone and noticed that he looked exhausted. She gently leaned in and kissed him on the forehead. "I think that's enough talking. You get some rest." She ran her fingers through his hair and smiled at him.

"So you've forgiven Daniel?"

"Yes. Just like I've forgiven you. I wrongly took my anger out on him, though, but I'm going to apologize for that right now. I'm going to call him and his mother and tell them how sorry I am. I'm also going to bake them a cake. You want to talk to him, too?"

"No," Lou replied. "No."

Lou's mom nodded. "Well, you think about what I said." She slowly walked out of his bedroom door.

As Lou lay down on his bed, a thousand feelings swept

90

over him. He couldn't control or understand them. He wanted to see his dad again. The strong emotion propelled him to go to the place where he and his father would spend some quiet "guy time" together—the rooftop.

Lou quietly slipped out the door. He strolled down the hall, entered the stairwell and climbed three floors to the roof's entrance and opened the door. Immediately, he was taken aback by the view before him. Beyond the clothesline and the wall, the view of thousands of twinkling city lights filled his eyes. It reminded him how much he loved living in the city. Car horns and traffic noise and other sounds of life filled the air. The sky was still dark and overcast and there was a strong breeze.

Lou parked himself in a secluded area on the roof where he and his dad used to sit together. He unleashed his thoughts and feelings. Memories flashed through Lou's mind like he was watching a home video. He saw himself with his dad playing catch, his dad teaching him to ride his bike, the expression on his father's face when he reeled in a huge trout, and his dad shaving. Lou then remembered the kind and gentle look in his father's eyes. Lou closed his eyes and in his mind heard his father's laugh. He took a deep breath in through his nostrils and remembered even the way his dad smelled. *I miss you so much, Dad. I miss you so much.* He bowed his head and wept.

CHAPTER TEN
The Big Game

Angry, frustrated, alone, Lou walked through the busy PS 132 halls like he didn't have a friend in the world. Suddenly, he heard his name being called from behind.

"Lou! Lou!" It was Miss Sandy.

Lou looked back and saw her running down the hall towards him.

"I've been looking for you!" she yelled.

Lou's eyes lit up. He knew what this could mean and he was still interested.

"I'm glad I caught you. I know you are anxious about this…"

Lou looked at her as if to say "Hurry, get to the point."

"First, I wanted you to know that I heard the kids talking about you and your baseball bat. Is… Is that why you wanted me to find that information… because you thought you had Lou Gehrig's bat?"

"Yeah," Lou confessed.

Miss Sandy hesitated. "Well, I'm afraid I don't have any great news for you. I checked… and there were four other students with the initials LG here during the time Lou Gehrig was here."

Lou bit his lip and glanced down.

"I'm sorry."

Lou raised his eyes and nodded, letting her know he was alright.

"What made you think it was Gehrig's bat anyway? Was his name on it?"

"Um. No. Just the initials LG hand carved on the bottom."

"Oh." She paused, thinking. "Maybe we could do a handwriting analysis of the initials... No. People don't carve the way they write." She paused again, thinking hard, then sighed. "I'm sorry. I just don't think there's any way we can really know. If there was only some way to prove... I wish..."

"That's all right," Lou overlapped. "I don't have the bat anymore anyway," Lou added, hoping to ease her shared frustration.

Miss Sandy gave him an awkward look.

"Mr. Townson has it. He said it was the school's property."

Miss Sandy nodded, "Oh really."

Lou didn't respond. He didn't want to get himself in any more trouble. Suddenly, the bell rang and all the students bustled to get to their classrooms.

"Well, I have to run. Sorry I didn't have good news for you, Lou." Miss Sandy turned and left.

"Hey, Lou!"

"Oh, man... Now what?" Lou asked himself. He had pumped himself up to do something and didn't like the disruptions. Lou turned around. It was Tanya.

94

"Did you hear the news?" she asked excitedly.

"No. What?" he said, despondently.

"Justin Rivers pitched a no hitter last night! That means you play the Braves in the championship next week."

"Wow." Lou said stunned.

"Justin's coach told everyone that since there was ample time for his arm to rest that he is going to pitch Justin again. *This* should be a really great game. I bet everyone's going to be there." Tanya's voice grew with enthusiasm.

Lou nodded, "Great." He looked inside his classroom and saw Mrs. Galarce taking attendance. He said goodbye to Tanya and aimed himself speedily for his desk. *Wow. A no hitter. That will surely feed his ego.* Huh, I should talk, he thought sarcastically.

Later that afternoon, Mr. Broom caught Lou in the hallway. He told Lou that he heard that the bat got him a lot of hits and that he was glad. He also heard the rumor that the bat might have belonged to Gehrig. Lou waited for him to say that he wanted the bat back, but Mr. Broom just smiled bigger and said, "I hope it really does belong to him. A good kid like you deserves a very special bat like that." Lou didn't have the heart to tell him the bat was no longer in his possession. Instead, he just said "thanks" and told Mr. Broom that he was a great guy.

As Lou walked home from school that day, he thought about what his mom had said to him. He still didn't know what he was going to do. *Today is the day I've been waiting for all my life—the championship!* He wondered why he didn't feel more excited about it. *I'll have to deal with Daniel. And Coach Jeffer still thinks I'm a jerk. And Justin is pitching. And I'm still in a slump.* Lou stopped there before his list of troubles got any larger and did damage to his psyche.

The championship game brought in a whole new flock of fans. Grandparents, brothers, sisters, aunts, uncles, friends, and local merchants joined parents. Almost every kid from the fifth and sixth grade was on hand as well. The fence surrounding the field was decorated with red, white and blue streamers. The smell of hot dogs and popcorn from street vendor carts floated through the park like a slow pop fly through the air.

If dreams could be recognized by a distinct smell, one could detect them in the air, as well. Joy shone in the eyes of every eleven and twelve-year-old boy on the field. The coaches and parents, too, carried themselves with a blend of childhood delight and nervousness at the importance of the event. No adult in the stands wanted to see his/her child's dream shattered when the last out was made. Yet, everyone knew there could only be one winner, and they hoped and prayed that it would be their child's team.

"Hey, can I talk to you for a minute?" It was Daniel.

Lou didn't respond. He shifted his weight awkwardly.

"Listen, I talked to your mom. We were glad she called. I- I-ah just want you to know that I'm sorry about what happened." Daniel unzipped his equipment bag. "My mom and dad offered to pay your mom for the bat, but she wouldn't accept our offer. I- I know nothing can replace your bat, but I wanted to give you this." He pulled out an old, wooden Louisville Slugger® baseball bat. "It's a Mickey Mantle model. It *wasn't* his though. It just has his name on it. It's from the 1950s." Daniel presented it to Lou. "Here."

Lou didn't take it. "This is pretty cool," he said, glancing at it in Daniel's hands. "You spent your own money?"

"Yeah, I got it at that memorabilia store on Sixth

96

Avenue. It's the same size as the other bat. The handle is a little thinner, but it still feels good. Take a swing."

Lou hesitated. He knew Daniel was saving up for a new trumpet and he was impressed by his sentiment. "Nah. That's all right." He looked Daniel in the eye. "Um… This is cool, but I think you should keep it. I think I've had it with wooden bats for a while." There was an awkward pause. "But, I… ah… want you to know that I… well… I forgive you, too. Apology accepted." Lou scratched the dirt with his cleat, then looked up and met eyes with Daniel. He stuck his hand out. "Friends?"

Daniel smiled and locked his hand in Lou's and they shook. "Friends. I don't blame you for being so mad."

Both boys nodded and drew an approved smile. The act of forgiving, it seemed, had the capacity for lifting a friendship to very high ground.

"Let's go Indians!" It was Coach Jeffer. He instructed his team to take the field for a pre-game warm up and batting practice. Afterward, Coach Jeffer rallied the Indians on their bench. Like the kids, he was thrilled to be there. It was amazing, he thought, that it was only a year ago that he often yelled 'Twenty two runs and we're back in this thing' to his team. He was proud of his boys and their accomplishment to say the least. They had come a long way to get to this moment.

Coach Jeffer reminded them what a fine group of boys they were, the finest he had ever coached. He also told them that even if the game ended without a victory, that they were still winners. He expressed his wish for everyone to relax and play good, solid, smart baseball and to have fun!

Everyone cheered anxiously. Coach Jeffer then read off

the game's line up. The batting order and field positions were as expected, except for one change: Lou's name was not mentioned.

At first Lou thought maybe he missed his name being called out, but then when he saw John Bailey, a reserve player, get excited and the other kids look at him, he knew his ears had been working properly. "Oh, man," Lou sighed. He swallowed a lump in his throat and tried not to look like it affected him. Lou knew a few of the players were examining him for just such a reaction.

Coach Jeffer told the team to "Get out there and win!" The Indians took the field.

Lou sat on the bench and watched. Ever since the first grade when Lou first started playing organized baseball, he dreamed of playing for a winning team and in a championship game. Though his face didn't show it, he was totally disappointed. Lou had wanted to apologize to the coach before the game, during batting practice and infield-outfield drills, but there was never an appropriate chance. Someone was always around. *You should have just done it. Maybe he would have played you.* He realized the game was about to start and his chance could soon be gone. He picked himself up and moved slowly toward Coach Jeffer. "Coach?"

"Hi, Lou,' Coach Jeffer answered awkwardly as he placed a copy of the line up on the clipboard that was mounted on the fence in front of the bench.

"Coach, I… I just wanted to apologize for what happened last week." Lou was spacing his words deliberately knowing he probably seemed shallow and maybe even manipulative. *He probably thinks I'm apologizing just so I can play.* "I raised my voice to you and didn't act like a man. I'm sorry. Oh, yeah… I'm also sorry for getting cocky and for hitting so bad." Lou stared at his cleats. He slowly looked up, as the coach cleared his throat.

"That's all right, Lou. Apology accepted."

A half smile formed on Lou's lips.

"I want you to know that you're not playing because of that. You're not concentrating when you get up there to hit. This is a big game, and I owe it to the team to field our best players. John's been hitting the ball solidly in practice lately. I …"

"I understand," admitted Lou, letting the coach off the hook.

Coach Jeffer smiled. Just then, the umpire called "Play ball!"

Lou turned on his heels and slowly walked back to the bench.

The Indians were the home team. From the moment of the first pitch it was immediately obvious that this was going to be a pitcher's duel. The Indian's pitcher, Darrell Jackson, gave up two hits in the first inning, but no runs scored.

Justin Rivers took the mound for the Braves each inning with intensity never before seen. He had a menacing look in his eyes. It was as if he hated the Indians more than he hated to lose. One by one he mowed them down and at the end of five innings, not a single batter had managed to get a hit off him. All those watching began quietly talking about the fact that Justin was possibly pitching another no hitter. As soon as it was mentioned, almost everyone abruptly ended talk of it for superstitious fear that talking about it might jinx it somehow.

On the Indians' bench Coach Jeffer had another plan.

"Men, gather 'round," he called. The team formed around him. "Listen, you can hit this guy. I know he's fast, but hang in there and get the bat on the ball. Justin Rivers out there is on the verge of making history and possibly tying a major league record that has never been tied."

Everyone's eyes lit up, especially Lou's.

"Only one man in the majors has ever pitched back to back no hitters. His name was Johnny Vander Meer, and it happened in Brooklyn in 1938 when he pitched for the Cincinnati Reds. It's one of the only major league records that will probably *never* be tied or broken."

"How do you know all this stuff?" queried Bobby in awe.

Coach Jeffer smiled his trademark smile. "That's why I'm The Coach." He paused, then- "Now, you guys aren't gonna let him tie that record… are ya?"

"No way!" each Indian declared in unison with a passion.

"I didn't think so. Now, be hitters in there." Coach Jeffer started to clap, a signal for everyone to disperse and get back in the game.

Richard Jeffer was a wise man and coach. His plan to tell his team about Vander Meer's record was twofold. First, he wanted to inspire them to get in the batter's box and fight. Second, he knew that he was probably one of the few people watching this game that actually knew about the record, and he hoped word of it would sneak to the Braves bench—and to Justin Rivers. It would be added pressure on the twelve-year-old, but this was war.

As the game continued, Coach Jeffer's pep talk, as inspirational as it was, did not prove to be effective. Justin would walk a batter here and there, but still no one

100

managed to get a hit or score a run. It was the bottom of the seventh inning. The score was 1 to 0 with the Braves in the lead. The Indians, still hitless, were up to bat. Tension filled the air and it started to show in Justin's pitching. With one out, he walked Bobby Darby with four wild pitches.

Due to the intense nature of the game, Lou was able to watch from the bench and cheer on his teammates without feeling sorry for not being part of the action. In a way, he felt sort of relieved that it would not be his strikeouts, ground balls or errors to put his team in jeopardy. It was much easier to watch his replacement feel the pressure than to be in there himself.

John Bailey stood outside the batter's box and looked for his signals from Coach Jeffer. Strangely, Coach Jeffer did nothing. He stood there frozen in a trance. John stared at him curiously, as did everyone else. Moments passed, then-

"Time!" The coach ran up to John and whispered to him. He then surveyed the bench as if he were scanning for some secret weapon in the last moments of battle. "Lou! You're up!"

What? Lou's mouth fell open and his stomach immediately started to turn like someone just switched on a washing machine inside him. He rose from the bench and stumbled toward the bats.

John brushed by him. "Good luck. You're gonna need it."

"Thanks." Lou found his black Easton bat and gripped it in his hands.

On the mound, Justin nodded and smiled like someone had just done him a tremendous favor. He threw the white pearl in and out of his glove with tremendous anticipation.

As Lou made his way toward home plate, he looked at

Coach Jeffer like he was looking at a lunatic. His heart raced. He'd never felt pressure like this in his life, not even when he tried to tie or break the record. His stomach was one big knot, and he longed to be sitting on the bench again watching John Bailey or anybody else up at bat.

Coach Jeffer's eye shone a spirit of confidence. "Be a hitter in there, Lou!" he clapped. "You can hit this turkey; I know it!" No signal was given, just clapping which meant 'get in there and hit.'

Lou took a deep breath and tried his best to focus. Immediately, his thoughts turned to the Spalding and he longed for it. Then, oddly, he looked at the Easton in his hands. He remembered that Christmas morning when he knew instantly that he had received a bat when he saw it under the tree. He then envisioned the expression on his mom's face when she saw how happy he was to unwrap it. He looked over his shoulder into the stands. There standing among the crowd was his mom. Her warm eyes imparted hope and let him know that she was with him. His thoughts quickly turned to his dad.

"Freakazoid!" echoed in the air. It was Andre Robinson, the Braves' second baseman.

The statement caused Justin to chuckle slightly on the mound.

Suddenly, the entire infield joined in a chorus of baseball chatter— "Freakazoid can't hit! Hey, freakazoid can't hit! No batta! No batta!"

Lou locked eyes with Justin who stared daggers at him.

With the tying run at first, Lou reminded himself to just make contact and try to advance the runner. Knowing Justin had a lightning quick fast ball, he dug his back foot deep into the rear of the batter's box. Justin wasted no time and delivered his pitch. Lou swung late and missed.

Ah! Wow! He is fast... Calm down... You can do this. Think. Think about something good. He looked at the black Easton. Instead of dwelling on his slump or the Spalding, he thought about his mom. His nerves settled a bit. In came the pitch. Lou swung and HIT it.

Foul ball!

The ball went sailing behind the third base bleachers.

"Foul tip!" Andre yelled with a laugh.

Justin received a new ball from his catcher. He looked encouraged that Lou barely got a piece of his pitch. He looked at Lou. It was as if their eyes were conversing with each other.

Okay. You got a piece of him. Now relax. Good mechanics... "Lord, I've never been much of a praying kid, but please help me," Lou said softly to himself. *No matter what happens I know you're with me.* Lou raised the black Easton above his shoulder. He envisioned his dad's laugh and smile. A feeling of peace overcame him.

Justin nervously looked in for the sign from the catcher. He started his wind up.

The crowd watching rose to their feet.

In came the pitch. It was going to be another strike. Lou shifted his weight and launched his swing-

PLINK!

The ball took off from the black Easton bat like it was jet propelled and sailed toward deep center field.

Everyone's feet and hearts jumped as Bobby Darby pumped his legs towards second base.

The center fielder sprinted to the wall.

Lou felt like he was in a slow motion dream again as he ran toward first looking out at center field.

The center fielder ran at top speed, his eyes focused on

103

the flying object like a retriever chasing a Frisbee. The ball went back... back... back... and headed over the fence. The center fielder leapt into the air, his glove going behind the wall with the ball. He hit the fence and tumbled to the ground.

Parents and coaches trembled at the impact and hoped he was all right. Suddenly, he rolled over and raised his glove high in the air! He opened it slightly and revealed the white ball!

Bobby jolted back toward first.

A mixture of cheers and guffaws filled the air.

Suddenly, Bobby touched first, tagged up and ran toward second. The center fielder quickly threw the ball to second. Bobby slid and was "Safe!"

Lou watched the action from first base in awe. He was thrilled, yet mad. He wanted to scream in frustrated anger and throw his helmet to the ground feeling robbed. Almost in shock, he didn't know what to do. Stunned by the play and stunned by the fact that he drilled the ball so far, he stopped his anger, composed himself and trotted slowly back toward the Indian bench.

Fans in the stands, his teammates and even a few kids on the Braves began to clap. A light applause perfumed the air. It made Lou's heart feel lighter and proud.

Lou locked eyes with his mom. Her eyes revealed her pride for his effort and actions. Lou returned her smile as he picked up his bat. He carried it with him to the bench and sat down.

Justin received the ball from the second baseman and approached the mound. He was now only one out from pitching back to back no hitters.

"Hey, that was some shot. I can't believe he caught it." Lou heard from out of nowhere. It was Doug.

Lou paused still in deep contemplation, then smiled. "I can take the good with the bad, though."

Doug did a double take. Meanwhile, Daniel stepped into the batter's box.

"Oh, man. I would not want to be him," Doug confessed.

The crowd in the park and on both benches stayed on their feet. This was the final showdown.

Beads of sweat formed on Daniel's and Justin's foreheads.

Nervously, Justin quickly worked the batter and threw two balls outside. His coach wasted no time and ran to the mound to calm his starting pitcher down. Justin said he was fine and that he wanted to continue. The next two pitches were perfect strikes, and Daniel swung his silver bat wildly at both.

His nerves taut like rubber bands, Daniel looked at Coach Jeffer for a sign. The coach wasted no time and clapped. Each clap seemed like exclamation points to silent prayers.

Daniel looked at Justin, who waited impatiently for him to get back into the batter's box. He didn't move, but stood there frozen either in fear or thought. He turned to the ump. "Time!" He looked like he was going to get sick. He trotted to the bench.

No one knew if he was going to ask for a pinch hitter or throw up. Coach Jeffer and his teammate's glared at him studying his every move.

Justin stood on the mound and shook his head. If this were a ploy to throw his timing off, he thought, it wouldn't work. It was only giving him more time to rest and regain his composure.

Daniel went straight to his equipment bag. He opened

it. The mouth of every Indian on the bench slowly dropped open as they watched Daniel pull out the *wooden* baseball bat. Daniel sighed with a sense of relief as he held the bat in his hands. Lou couldn't believe what he was seeing.

"Oh, no… Not again." It was Frank. "Whose bat was that? Babe Ruth's?" he asked half-joking.

Daniel smiled. "Nope. It's mine." Unsteadily, he held the Louisville Slugger out in front of him for all eyes to see and aimed himself for home plate. He was still nervous and it showed in his awkward walk.

The bench was speechless. As Daniel looked for a sign, they started to cheer him on with tremendous enthusiasm. For some strange reason, the interruption gave everyone on the Indians an increased feeling of hope. Maybe it was because of the old Spalding. Maybe it was because of the look in Daniel's eyes. Whatever it was didn't matter. They clapped and cheered their teammate on with everything they had. "Come on, Danny baby! You can do it!"

Daniel stared into Justin's eyes and raised the wooden Louisville Slugger above his shoulder.

"Come on, Daniel! You can do it!" Lou shouted with all his heart.

The cheering from both benches was so loud one could barely hear himself think.

The count was two and two and there were two outs. Bobby, the tying run, jumped anxiously up and down at second. Justin wound up and delivered his pitch. Daniel gritted his teeth and swung with all his might-

CRACK!

He made contact with the ball.

Andre Robinson took off and ran from his position at second into right field… He dove! As he hit the ground, the ball dropped between him and the right fielder for a clean hit.

Bobby rounded third and headed for home. The right fielder bobbled the ball, then came up throwing. Bobby slid as the catcher caught the ball and turned for the tag. It was going to be close…

"Safe! The umpire yelled.

The score was tied. The catcher began arguing with the ump. All the while, at Coach Tilly's instruction, Daniel was running. The catcher quickly heard his teammates screaming and saw Daniel half way between second and third. He ran at Daniel, who froze for a split second, then took off like a bandit toward third. The catcher rushed his throw and overthrew third base. Everyone went crazy and yelled as Daniel touched third base and was waved home by Coach Jeffer. He ran as fast as his skinny legs would carry him. The left fielder retrieved the ball and threw it with all his might toward home. Daniel threw his legs forward and launched his slide as the ball hit the catcher's glove. A cloud of dust filled the air as they collided. A brief moment passed, that seemed like minutes to all watching.

"S-a-a-a-f-e!" the umpire called.

Cheers came from one side of the field, screaming and arguing on the other.

The Indians leapt into the air and piled on top of Daniel. It was the greatest moment of their lives. Coaches Jeffer and Tilly joined the pile.

Justin hung his head low. A tear ran down his face as he and his teammates dragged themselves off the field. Andre and a few of the other Braves players cried as well.

Lou ran up to Daniel and gave him a high five. "That was awesome!"

"Tell me about it," Daniel replied.

A smile jumped from Daniel's face to Lou.

Bobby picked up the wooden Louisville Slugger and handed it to Daniel. "Dude, it's cracked. Too bad."

"Hey, good thing it did," interrupted Coach Tilly, among the congratulating. "If that had been an aluminum bat, that hit would have been an easy pop fly to right." His smile launched others.

Daniel still beamed. "That's all right. I'll get another one." He turned to Lou. "Maybe in a hundred years some kid will find my bat." He showed Lou the bottom of the bat where he had penned the initials DE.

The team celebrated. As parents, friends and family ran onto the field, some of the Indians humorously stated they were all going to get wooden bats.

Lou looked into the stands and saw his mom. Tears were running down her cheeks. It was the first time he had seen her cry since his father passed away.

Full of pride, Daniel's dad ran onto the field and embraced him. Lou watched and wished his own father could take him into his arms. He wondered if his dad was watching him from heaven. He looked up at the sky and smiled.

Soon thereafter, the league director started the awards ceremony. First and second place trophies were given to each player. It was Lou's very first trophy, and he couldn't wait to put it on his dresser. He raised it proudly to his mom, watching in the stands. Beaming, she clapped and gave him the thumbs up.

The ceremony ended and everyone headed for home. Like all good soldiers after an intense battle, players, coaches and parents on both sides were happy it was over—and tired.

CHAPTER ELEVEN
Extra Inning

Lou took the wooden baseball bat mounting brackets, which he bought at a local sporting goods store, and carefully screwed them both into the wall with his mom's electric screwdriver. With a half-smile, he then gently placed the old, wooden Spalding on its new home. He stepped down from his bed and admired his work. *Perfect. That looks great.*

Just a few hours earlier, Mr. Townson had given the bat back to Lou. It seems Mr. Townson had a nice little conversation with Miss Sandy, or rather, she had a conversation with him. During her "talk," she told him about her research, the four other people with the initials LG, and that the bat probably didn't belong to Lou Gehrig after all. Mr. Townson asked Lou to keep the matter confidential. Thrilled to have the bat back in his ownership, Lou agreed with not another thought about the matter. He was thankful to say the least.

It was a good day for Lou. He also received a brand new pair of sneakers during school from Justin Rivers.

Justin, it seemed, may not always be nice, but he kept his word. The sneakers, which were just like Justin's, fit perfectly. Since he was robbed of a homerun, they were a nice alternative reward for hitting the ball off Justin, Lou thought.

Lou glanced at the championship trophy sitting next to his two game balls on the dresser. He reflected on all that had happened during the past few weeks. It was amazing, he thought, that a 30-inch hunk of wood from a white ash tree carved into a cylinder to form a baseball bat could have had such an impact on his life. All the hitting glory he received, though it lasted only a brief time, felt good, but being part of a winning team and having stronger friendships felt better.

The kids at PS 132 saw a change in Lou—in his words, his actions and even in how he carried himself. All they had to do was ask him and he would have told them the reason for his change. Curiosity got the best of some and they did ask. Others, simply watched from a distance and made their own erroneous assumptions as to why Lou walked a little taller now.

Lou didn't care that the bat probably wasn't the property of Gehrig. For him, the bat was a tool used in his journey of discovering truth. Much like the way a bat drives a ball into play where a myriad of wonderful and exciting things can happen in a game, this bat drove events in Lou's life forward. He liked the way his life was being put into play, and he knew that no matter what happened, good or bad, his faith in the Lord, just like his dad believed, would see him through. Just like in baseball, every day was like a new game. For Lou, it was a game—and a journey—which had only just begun.

Post Game
Wrap Up

Lou Gibson and his Spalding bat had one more game to be played! Two weeks after the championship game, the Gibson's phone rang. It was Miss Sandy. She told Lou she just couldn't get the bat out of her mind and had spent hours searching through old files looking for some way to trace the bat to Gehrig. She had practically given up when she stumbled upon an old file of photos. Inside the folder were seven very old photos from the early 1900s. Three of the seven photos had Lou Gehrig in them. One photo depicted Gehrig with three other boys, all wearing baseball uniforms—and Gehrig was holding a bat!

Lou's heart hammered inside him as he heard Miss Sandy speak. He immediately invited her over and within an hour she was at the door. Lou and his mom greeted Miss Sandy politely, but Lou could barely control himself. Miss Sandy quickly and carefully pulled the photo from the manila folder and handed it to Lou. Lou examined it closely and screamed. "It's there! It's there! It's the bat! It's the bat!" He jumped up and down. "It's the bat! I knew it! I knew it all the time!"

"Are you sure?" asked his mom. Her knees were flexing. She was practically starting to jump with him.

Miss Sandy's smile grew larger and larger.

"Yes! The mark! That black spot on the bat. It's there. The Spalding logo is the same. It's the bat! The picture proves it!" Lou jumped up and down. He didn't know what to do with himself. He wanted to run around the room.

Lou's mom jumped, too.

"This is so exciting," said Miss Sandy energetically. "Lou, may I see the bat?"

"Sure." Lou ran into his room.

Lou's mom and Miss Sandy exchanged thrilled and excited looks.

Lou ran back and handed Miss Sandy the bat and the photo. She carefully studied them both. Her grin widened. "Looks like a match to me."

"Yes! Thank you so much!" howled Lou's mom.

"Yeah! Thank you!" followed Lou. "Without you, we never would have been able to prove it."

"You're welcome. I'm- I'm just as excited as you are. This was the toughest research project I ever had. It was a miracle that I even found that folder."

"Well, you're talking to two people who believe in miracles," said Lou's mom. "And we sure needed one like this."

Miss Sandy took a few swings with the bat and let out a burst of joyful laughter.

They all celebrated with some cookies and chocolate milk. Miss Sandy told the Gibson's that she had a friend named Carl Nellis who was a researcher at Sotheby's, the world-famous auction house. She told them that she believed the bat could bring in a lot of money at an auction and that they should seriously think about whether or not they would want to sell the bat.

It was a thought that had already crossed both their minds. However, the decision was up to Lou. Lou certainly had a big decision to make, and he and his mom both prayed for guidance.

Lou sat next to his mom in the audience on the day of the big auction. As soon as bidding opened, the room went crazy with excitement as bid after bid after bid took place. It was obvious that many people wanted to own the one and only Spalding baseball bat once owned by Lou Gehrig as a boy.

There were bidders in the room and individuals bidding on phone lines. Lou and his mom reveled in the feverish frenzy as the price of the bat went from $10,000 to $20,000 to $25,000 to $30,000... Suddenly, Lou's mom felt like she was going to faint, but she regained her composure as the next bid for $35,000 was waved.

The bidding continued... Lou didn't know what to think. His entire being felt numb as bidder after bidder raised a higher bid. The bidding—and the tension in the room—grew higher and higher, until...

"We have $67,000," the auctioneer proclaimed. "Any higher bids?" There was a pause as all eyes scanned the room. "Going once for $67,000. Going twice..." He took his gavel and paused, then hammered the podium. "SOLD! For $67,000!"

Applause filled the room as everyone stood up. Miss Sandy ran to Lou and his mom and hugged them. "Thank you, Lord!" Lou's mom screamed with joy and jumped up and down like she had just won the lottery, which in a way, she had. She picked up her son and hugged him wildly. The clapping continued.

The winning bidder, a young Internet entrepreneur,

approached the podium and claimed his prize. He picked up the bat and examined it carefully. His smile widened as he read the Spalding logo and studied the initials LG on the bottom of the handle. He then looked at the photo of Gehrig, which came with the bat, and compared the two. He nodded approvingly. His smile grew even wider as he waved everyone back, then took a walloping Gehrig style swing.

Camera flashes went off as photographers from all the major newspapers captured the moment forever.

Lou watched the commotion as if it were an out of body experience and not really happening to him. Being so young, he couldn't fully appreciate how much money $67,000 really was, but he knew it was a lot. I wonder how much it would have gone for if it was not cracked, he thought.

Photographers approached him and asked him to hold the bat with its new owner. As more camera flashes went off, Lou looked at the bat as if to say goodbye. He was impressed with how well Sotheby's professional had repaired and restored the bat. The crack was visible, but barely. Lou touched the bat one last time. He never imagined it could be worth so much money to anyone. For him the bat represented a tremendous learning experience, which, he thought, was probably why God brought the bat into his life.

Lou and his mom already discussed how they would spend the money, never imagining there would actually be so much to allocate. Lou decided that ten percent would immediately be given to their church and to the local homeless shelter to help feed the poor. Two thousand dollars would be given to Mr. Broom, the janitor, as a way of thanking him for the gift of the bat. Another two thousand dollars would be given to Miss Sandy for her role in helping Lou discover that it was Gehrig's bat after all. The balance would be used to pay off some bills and invested for Lou's future college tuition. Maybe I'll even go to Columbia University like Gehrig, Lou thought.

Lou's thoughts then turned to the kids at school. *Maybe I'll buy everyone lunch. They're gonna freak out when they find out about this!* Lou then thought about the importance of his actions and words regarding what had just transpired. He would make sure not to act cocky. Lou felt a real appreciation for how one life can impact another.

As the last photo was taken, Lou watched his hand let go of the old, wooden Spalding baseball bat. He thought back to how a simple case of laughter and the giggles brought the bat into his life. That reflection caused him to giggle again as his mom shot him a proud and happy smile. It seemed that with a new understanding about the power of forgiveness and $67,000 now headed for a new bank account in his name, that Lou Gibson had the last laugh after all.

Fact vs. Fiction

It has been said that the truth is sometimes stranger than fiction. With that in mind, I wanted to share the elements in *Hitting Glory* that are true and set them apart from what was merely created in my imagination.

Fact:

• Lou Gehrig did attend PS 132 in New York, New York. He was graduated in 1917.

• Spalding made baseball bats in the late 1800s and throughout the 1900s. Spalding, along with the A.J. Reach Company, J.F. Hillerich & Co. and J.W. & Company, was one of the first large companies to produce baseball bats and equipment.

• Lou Gehrig was born on June 19, 1903.

• Gehrig's favorite player was Honus Wagner, a famous short stop in the early 1900s. Gehrig liked him because he was also a German immigrant.

• Gehrig did attend Commerce High School where he never missed a day of school.

• Gehrig did attend Columbia University where he was a star football and baseball player before he became a Yankee.

• Gehrig did have a hard working mom who worked as a cook at Columbia. She wanted her son Lou to go to college to become an engineer and for him to be successful.

• Gehrig batted over .300 12 straight times, led the American League in home runs three times, led the American League in RBIs five times, and played on six World Championship teams.

• Gehrig played in 2,130 consecutive games, a feat that won the first baseman the nickname "The Iron Horse." The record stood until 1995. On September 5 and 6 at Oriole Park at Camden Yards against the California Angels, Cal Ripken became baseball's all-time "Iron Man" tying and breaking Lou Gehrig's consecutive games record.

• Lou Gehrig died on June 2, 1941. He had amyotrophic lateral sclerosis, a rare muscle disease that took his life at the age of 37.

• Johnny Vander Meer is the only pitcher in Major League baseball history to have thrown back-to-back no-hitters. The 23-year-old rookie southpaw accomplished the feat on the very first night game at Ebbetts Field, with Babe Ruth and hundreds of people from Vander Meer's hometown, Midland Park, NJ, in attendance. The first no-hitter occurred on June 11, 1938 against the Boston Braves. The second occurred four days later on June 15 against the Dodgers. In his next start, "Vandy" didn't allow a hit until Boston's Deb Garms singled in the fourth inning, ending the record of hitless innings at 21!

118